Colorado Mountain WOMEN

TALES FROM THE MINING CAMPS

BY SHERIE FOX SCHMAUDER

Persevere!
Sherie Fox Schmauder
To Linda
Keep on
going
always!

WESTERN REFLECTIONS
PUBLISHING COMPANY®

Lake City, Colorado

ACKNOWLEDGEMENTS:
"The Terrible Weight of Snow" was originally published in *U. S. 1 Worksheets*, Volume 40/41, 1999, published by the U.S. 1 Poets' Cooperative, Princeton, NJ, P.O. Box 127, Kingston, NJ, 08528-0127.

DISCLAIMER

This book is a work of fiction. Names, characters, places and incidents are used fictitiously or are the products of the author's imagination. Any resemblance to actual events, locales or people, living or dead, is entirely coincidental.

ISBN: 978-1-890437-80-0

Library of Congress Control Number: 2003102282

Cover and text design by Laurie Goralka Design
Cover photo: Laurie Goralka Casselberry

Third Edition
Printed in the United States of America

Western Reflections Publishing Company®
P.O. Box 1149
951 N. Highway 149
Lake City, CO 81235
www.westernreflectionspub.com

This book is dedicated to my parents, Joseph J. Fox and Helen Anderson Fox, and to my son, Jonathan F. Schmauder, who took me on the odyssey that led to these stories.

I would especially like to thank Debbie Brockett, Jane B. Rawlings, Lea Wait, Norma Sheard, Louise Liebold and Marlow Schmauder for their invaluable editorial help. Members of the U.S. 1 Poets' Collective in Princeton, NJ, gave traditionally rigorous editorial suggestions on some of the earlier stories.

Table of Contents

Introduction

INTRODUCTION

*M*ining camps all over the early West were grim places. People had to cope with bone-chilling cold and suffocating snows in the high mountains. Some miners froze to death; others lost limbs from frostbite. Starvation in the mountain winters was a distinct possibility.

Cave-ins happened all the time, at any altitude. Sometimes trapped miners on small, isolated claims were not missed for months, if at all. The only way to dig out victims was with determination, shovels, and incredible strength. Sometimes mines flooded, overwhelming men and their pack animals without warning.

Living conditions were primitive, even in tent cities that sprang up wherever miners found a very rich strike. Some boom towns had real buildings that helped keep people warm in the winter, but many small strike areas never grew that civilized.

Some men worked in the same clothing for months, until it rotted or shredded and fell off. Why care about your clothes when there was gold to be dug out or panned? If you didn't work as fast as you could, someone else might find your gold, even if you had staked a claim. Men could be killed for their claims. Grizzlies and mountain lions didn't take kindly to invaders of their turf.

♛

Women who went to Colorado mining camps in the late 1800s and early 1900s were survivors. The cold, stark realities of the hostile environment toughened them up. Raising children and helping others even worse off than themselves made them even tougher.

But sometimes they cracked.

The women I write about in this book are distillations, imaginations of real women and what the wilderness might have done to them. Their strength of character and of body affected those around them.

Some women came to the mining camps alone because they wanted to. They loved the mountains and life away from civilization. Many wives came with their treasure-obsessed husbands, possibly not by their own choice. Some men actually hit paydirt and gave their wives lives of ease. Most did not.

Other women came to the mining camps as prostitutes. Many found it the only way to make a living in the harsh world of the mining camps. Some chose that life because they loved it. Sometimes children were sold into that sordid, painful world. Disease killed men, women and children in the camps, being more partial to taking children.

Colorado Mountain Women is a collection of quintessential fictional renderings of women who civilized the West. That vast area could not have progressed without the courage, strength and determination of such women.

The Terrible
Weight of Snow

ONE
The Terrible Weight of Snow

he snow. In September when it first fell, I was delighted — so feathery, each flake unique on my black woolen mittens. No snow back in Charleston, where dear Mama would have fainted at the thought of her only daughter now living in this crude Colorado mining camp high above the rest of the world. (Henry had been so charming in those days, so fiery as he told of the riches to be won in the uncharted West. He had won us both.)

By December — when Henry grumbled daily at having to shovel the snow from our little cabin to the privy — I quailed. His fits of anger came more often, as if I were the source of the cold, heavy snow driving now straight down, now horizontally in the slashing wind.

Lately I have spent much time mopping up food he flings from the table. We have no crockery left, only tin plates. The other wives here know little more than I of making various beans and preserved meats palatable.

The wind never stops here, 10,000 feet and more above Charleston, so far to the east. The pines moan even in our sheltered glade. But at least in my cabin, away from the edge of the precipice, I am safe from the awful views of the cold mountains across the empty valley. I don't have to watch the aerial tram cars full of ore make their dizzying descent to the main road, then rocket upward empty and creaking.

It is January now, and the windows are covered, the snow over six feet deep. In blizzards the men walk a rope to the mine, its length strung tree to tree, ever higher as the snow deepens. Henry would keep only that one window cleared, not just for my sake, but for others walking in the night who depend on the glow to find their way to warmer homes than mine. I am left alone in our tiny cabin most of each day, so I sit by the front window knitting or reading my few books over and over by the fitful light between storms. I can do nothing useful here at all.

The mules can't drag the sleds when the drovers cannot see through the swirling snow. There is the precipice. After new snow the animals sink to their bellies and flounder. I am like those animals.

Supplies should come up on sledges when the weather clears. What will they carry down the mountain the next time?

So heavy the snow; it builds in drifts over the cabin tops and sometimes the roofs collapse. It takes the men from the mine to rescue the women and children. Or to bury them. Afterwards, Tongrief, the foreman, weights the men with more work to make up the lost time. Dig faster! Use more dynamite in each blast! Has the man no compassion for the widower?

♛

Yesterday Henry tripped running from the set dynamite charge. The mass of fallen rock held his legs, crushed his hip. The men carried him back here on a door, the weight of him making them sweat in their muffled woolens.

He now lies in our bed groaning, gasping for relief, even through the laudanum and the liquor. He swears at me while I sit silently at my window. I cannot help him. My headache rages from the coal fumes rising from the black iron stove; it pounds with a heavy hammer on the anvil of my mind.

♛

Several hours ago I realized that new snow had partly clogged the tin chimney. Smoke dropped heavily and oozed from the cracks around the closed stove door.

I pulled Henry's mine-filthy coat over my black winter dress, wrapped my head in the red wool muffler dear Mama knitted for me, put on boots. I knew I must clear the drifted snow from the path around the house and fight my way up the ladder nailed to the house on the downwind side. Henry will no longer be able to keep the snow clear, and the other men are busy with their own homes.

I can scarcely bear the thought of what I will have to do to survive this winter.

I looked at my work-ruined hands, the cracked skin around each nail, before I pulled on my mittens and picked up the heavy shovel.

If I left snow clogging the chimney through this coming night of storm, and if I stoked the stove to keep the ice thin in the water pail and frostbite away from us both while we slept, the fumes might reach Henry in his bed and me by my window.

So I climbed the ice-encrusted wooden ladder with numb hands, the snow falling heavily. My breath was white and frozen in the keening wind. The ladder shook as the sharp wind pierced my clothing.

As I struggled with the heavy snow on the roof I thought of how I had strolled under the moss-laden trees of Charleston with my girlhood friends, our fans moving the humid air, our thin muslin dresses cool on our hot young bodies. Tears froze on my chapped face.

In the spring, perhaps before June, when surely the incredible weight of snow will have melted and been transmuted into clear running water flowing down and down from this awful mountain fastness, I will leave this place. I shall leave Henry, buried in the glade back by the little lake where we picnicked in the green summer. I will go back to life where there is no terrible weight of snow and of other things.

Behind Lace Curtains

TWO
Behind Lace Curtains

*T*his is what Susanna saw from behind her lace curtains, the ones she had brought with her from St. Louis along with a secret supply of drawing tablets: Mr. Douglas, walking with measured tread from the bank to the post office. A quick sketch on her open drawing pad captured his self-importance, his closed features.

Next she saw Evangeline Edgars, her posture very erect, walking quickly from her house up the street. She also entered the post office. That was an easy sketch, Susanna thought, smiling. A few lines suggested Evangeline's reticence at collecting attention as well as her strict upbringing. You could always tell by the posture how cared for, how relaxed and satisfied with one's self a person was.

Soon two little boys darted by, playing hoops in the middle of the street, dodging horses and wagons as if they were no more than flies to avoid. Susanna had to sketch quickly to catch the motion, the concentration, the determination of each to outdo the other in daring. One would dash close to a horse or a wagon, make the hoop turn and a collision of the two boys seem inevitable, then veer off crying, "Almost gotcha that time!"

Susanna's attention wandered back to the post office, where Mr. Douglas and Evangeline Edgars came out of the door more or less together. Mr. Douglas, with that nonchalant courtesy of his, held the door open for Evangeline Edgars. But now Evangeline looked somehow different. A delicate joy lit her thin face, and she smiled at Mr. Douglas. Had she received a letter with good tidings? Perhaps her folks back East had written?

Susanna's pencil flew over a fresh page. She barely looked at her drawing. Later, when she was out of her subject's intense emotional aura, Susanna would find that her fingers had captured the true essence of the woman, the one she didn't want anyone to know.

Seeing the inner reality of people was Susanna's desperate secret.

No, it couldn't have been a letter from parents. Evangeline Edgars had been orphaned some years ago. She'd said as much when she moved to St. Elmo two years ago. Then what?

Mr. Douglas? Surely not! How could anything be going on there? Susanna would surely know about it. Susanna knew everyone's past in the town, she thought. But then again . . .

A gentle breath of air from up this narrow forested valley fluttered the lace curtains in the open bay windows. Susanna was momentarily distracted by their white filigreed beauty. When she focused again on the pair at the post office, they had parted ways. Damn! She had missed a telling scene. (What would Stanley think if he ever knew she cursed on occasion! But he never would — words like that only slipped out when she drew people, and she never sketched when Stanley was in the house.)

A shriek rent the air. One of the little boys was down, a passing wagon wheel rolling over his small body.

Did she need to go help?

Poor lamb, he was still lying there crying lustily, under the wagon between the front and back wheels. Susanna sat back a bit, and her pencil flew over the paper. The man in the wagon had stopped his horses quickly, and the animals were now shuffling and tossing their heads, upset with the commotion behind them.

The child was alive, that was good. Evangeline Edgars had rushed to him, even if she wasn't his mother. She had no children, and with her husband off in the diggings most of the time she would have none in the near future. Now a crowd was forming. Doc Packard came running with his little black bag.

Susanna flipped the page, capturing Evangeline Edgars, her horrified concern warring with her obvious desire to do the right thing in such a dreadful incident. The frantic driver. The nervous horses. The hysterical mother. Doc Packard with his air of total competence.

Then they were all gone: the boy carried off by the doctor, one leg already splinted and bound up with white bandages, his mother accompanying them, looking furious. Susanna closed her sketch pad and went to make a cup of coffee. She fortified it with whiskey.

Trembling slightly, she opened today's first page of sketches. She had never meant to know everyone's hidden thoughts, but her hands drew them. She had never meant to see into the deeper realms of humanity. Still she had to look, had to know.

That was why she had been turned out of her own home in St. Louis. She had always had this frightening ability to see beneath the public surface of people with her pencil.

Mama had seen Susanna's sketch of her with Mr. Bonden. They had only been having tea, she had cried, and she had hit Susanna hard enough to send her reeling across the room. "How could you draw such vile expressions?" she demanded. "What would your father say?" She'd nearly fainted as she leafed through Susanna's sketches of the lust-driven servants' faces, of her own friends' envious and greedy expressions while they sat in her parlor sipping tea and eating little cookies and petits fours. The drawing of Papa had been the final blow. Mama had to lean back on the settee after she looked at that, her eyes closed, fanning herself frantically with a lace hankie, trying to recover herself.

Mama had burned that sketch right then, and the sketchbook too. No one could look at a book that had been burned.

Susanna had been confined to her room most of the time then, forbidden to draw. Papa was told Susanna had formed an unsavory acquaintance and could not be trusted to go out of the house until a suitable marriage had been arranged. Stanley had pretended to be suitable, had made Susanna's parents believe he was already a millionaire, with vast silver mines. He wanted a society wife, he said, for entertaining investors in Denver.

And here she was in St. Elmo, behind her lace curtains. She had never seen an investor from Denver come here.

Stanley would never see her drawings. She burned them herself.

Being in secluded St. Elmo, where there were more miners than merchants, and more scarlet daughters of prosperity than wives, had developed Susanna's powers of seeing through people to a shocking degree. She'd decided it must be the altitude and the clean air (not counting the dust of Main Street). Most people who chose to live here and pursue activities to do with mining had no pretenses. That helped too.

And the trees: the pine trees, the aspens, the junipers, the firs. Susanna especially loved the way tall pines, with their rough dark trunks, made such an intense contrast to aspens, with their smooth white trunks. She thought of them as masculine and feminine; complimenting and necessary to each other. In St. Louis there were not so many trees. Trees spoke to Susanna, and they nurtured her. They took away the sordid aspect of her drawing people without their skins. Susanna walked out of town daily, usually right after Stanley left for the mine, even before she did her housework. She talked to the trees. In their presence she felt that her gift was accepted as long as she used it for good.

On the occasions when she found something good and striking about people, she managed to tell them about it, to compliment them in such a way that they never imagined how she knew their character. But usually what she found had to be kept secret. Most people never looked deeply into themselves, and would be shocked by Susanna's knowledge. She smiled at those people, and was silent.

Now she steeled herself to look at the sketches of Evangeline Edgars and Mr. Douglas. But it wasn't what she thought. The two were brother and sister! Why was this a secret?

To be sure, Evangeline Edgars had a lover. Did *Mr.* Edgars know any of this? Not likely, she thought with a small smile.

Who?

Susanna's next days were frantic, spent sketching every moment when Stanley was off at his mine. She sketched everyone who passed. She drew multiple sketches of Evangeline

Edgars when she walked by on her way to the mercantile. And again when she walked back to her home. Susanna wanted to know who Evangeline's lover was.

On Sunday, Susanna and Stanley went to church. Evangeline Edgars was there with her husband, her black hair upswept under a modest hat, veil lowered against the mosquitoes that darted invisibly through the opened windows. Susanna's fingers itched to draw; here were more townspeople than passed her lace-curtained windows in a whole day. They hid stories that screamed to be sketched, she was sure.

She realized this morning she had seldom sketched Reverend Peters. And she had always definitely avoided drawing Stanley. She couldn't bear to find out anything sordid about this man to whom she was bound for her natural life. He had already lied about his prospects as a miner. What else might he be hiding?

After the service, Stanley said he was going to talk about some mine equipment with Mr. Douglas. He would need a loan. Susanna frowned. She was already making do with less and less money each month for the household and food. How could they pay off another loan?

Susanna chatted aimlessly with several friends, including Evangeline, then hurried home to set a small piece of pork to roast for Sunday dinner. Stanley still wasn't home, so she dared take from her sewing basket a small sketchpad. People were still passing by, strolling in the summer's heat. She drew groups of people. She caught every man, including Reverend Peters, and most of the women, including Evangeline, who walked with two other women. She hadn't thought Reverend Peters was as good-looking as her fingers seemed to notice today. She would look at him more closely later.

Stanley finally came up the street, tipping his hat to friends, speaking a word and continuing on. Hidden behind her lace curtains and fighting against her better judgment, she did a quick sketch of him with others, then a last hasty one as he turned in the gate.

She was shaking as she quickly hid the pad in her sewing basket. She had never dared to draw when he was so near.

He came into the room. "What is that good smell? Pork roast? I hope you put potatoes in the pan to suck up some of that good juice."

"Of course," she said, standing up abruptly and turning to go check on the roast.

Her quick motion was her undoing. In her haste, the sewing basket had not been placed securely on the table. It tumbled off, spilling threads, scissors, thimble, pins and needles, pencil . . . sketchbook.

She couldn't hide the book fast enough.

"What have we here?" asked her husband as he gently took the book from her suddenly nerveless hand.

Susanna could only stand silently, lifeless, as Stanley flipped though the pages one by one. The color drained from his face.

He held the small booklet out to her, opened to one page. "How could you ever imagine such wild things? Do you have so much time on your hands that you make up vicious stories with your pencil?"

She swayed and glanced down to see what she — and her husband — had discovered. It was the one of Stanley tipping his hat to Evangeline. The leer on his face was shocking. One hand was at his swollen crotch. In the background was Mr. Douglas, a look of hatred distorting his face.

Stanley spoke out again. "That you should imagine Mr. Douglas hates me is one thing, but you are completely unhinged to think I harbor such thoughts about Miss Edgars. Perhaps Mr. Douglas is her lover, is that it?

"We should think about what to do with you," he continued, staring at her with a cold, closed look. "Now that I think about it, your parents seemed quite indecently relieved when I offered for your hand. What did they know that I didn't?"

Susanna's hand was at her throat, a feeling of suffocation closing in on her. But then a small core of iron seemed to shore up her wilting body. Her sketches must have some good purpose. They must. Yet two times now they had changed her life for the worse.

Her heart became hard. Why was she quailing? *He* was the one who had strayed.

But her husband could have her locked up as a hysterical madwoman. That happened to women sometimes.

Perhaps she would have an ally in Mr. Douglas.

A sudden wind came up and rattled the windows in their frames. The lace curtains rippled in the air currents and obscured the view for a moment, then parted briefly and gave Susanna a clear glimpse of the trees on the hillside beyond the town.

Maybe she would take the lace curtains down from the windows in this house in St. Elmo and put them up in another house. Somewhere else with trees. A place of her own. Susanna could draw an excellent portrait when she looked at her work as she drew. People would pay her for their true likenesses. Especially if she edited out their flaws.

She could do that.

Naomi and Ruth

THREE
Naomi and Ruth

*W*here was Frank? He wasn't waiting for Naomi at the Leadville train station. She sighed and set her mouth, putting her satchel down so she could shift the baby to the other arm. That was Frank, all right, not remembering the date. She had written him a month ago that she would travel as soon as she had recovered from the birth. Could the mails have been held up? She smiled at the nice young woman who had kept her company from Denver, then frowned a little as a carriage full of fancy women pulled up. The woman from the train gave a cry of delight and ran to them, and was soon enveloped in their laughing midst.

Well, she must learn to get along with things as they were here in this raw western town. There would be all kinds of things she would have to get used to. Leadville certainly wasn't civilized, but that didn't mean it would be bad. Frank would help her adjust to life in the mountains.

Naomi could scarcely see where to go for all the wagons full of building supplies, the horses dashing here and there, the sorry-looking prospectors heading downhill with burros struggling under loads of mining supplies. She looked around through the gently falling snow, trying to decide where to look for Frank.

Little Josie stirred in her sleep as a flake landed on her little cheek. Naomi jiggled her a bit to keep her quiet. She stood beside her big satchel and looked at her trunk sitting forlornly on the platform. She must locate Frank right away, and get Josie and herself into shelter before the snow became thicker.

That night she was lucky to find a tiny room at a nearby hotel close to the Tabor Grand Opera House. Naomi hoped Frank had taken a liking to opera and would escort her to some of the performances. But now her problem was how to find Frank. No one she asked had heard of Frank Heffron.

The next day Naomi decided to ask at the mercantiles that were interspersed among the saloons and gambling clubs. In and out she went, Josie getting heavier in her arms as her skirt hem became even heavier with snow. Ice slicked the boardwalks from last night's storm, making her trek dangerous. The high altitude left her feeling lethargic, and she had to force herself to go on.

She was in the last grocery store on the street and just about to give up when she heard a woman's voice say, "Please charge that to Mrs. Frank Heffron's account."

Shocked, Naomi spun around. Who was using her name? *She* was Mrs. Frank Heffron, not that woman, pleasant as she looked. The woman started past Naomi on her way out the door, and impulsively Naomi put out her gloved hand.

"Excuse me, ma'am, but I don't see how there can be two Frank Heffrons. I am Mrs. Frank Heffron, and I've come with our baby from Illinois to join him."

Naomi had spoken quietly, not wanting to create a scene, but still the woman's face went white and she looked as if she would faint. She leaned back on the counter.

"He told me you were dead," she whispered.

Naomi was astonished. "Obviously I am not dead. If he married you, then he is a bigamist! I know Frank is a little flighty, always chasing after one get-rich scheme or another, but how could he do this to both of us?" She looked closely at the woman, who seemed a very decent sort. "What are we to do?"

The woman recovered a little at these firm words. "Come home with me. People mustn't hear us. Frank is off at his claim and won't be back for two or three days." She looked down at sleeping Josie then, and Naomi saw tears in her eyes.

"And the baby — what a beautiful baby. I don't seem to be able . . ."

She blushed, and Naomi understood what she meant. She offered a better look at the peaceful baby, who obligingly opened her blue eyes and gave a little yawn before falling asleep again.

Ruth Heffron took Naomi's arm on the icy wooden side-walk, and they walked away from the main part of town until they came to a small, well-kept cabin.

Once inside, with strong coffee fortifying both women, the decision was made. Ruth went to her husband's strong box, which he kept under the bed, and with the aid of a slim knife managed to open the lock.

Inside was a divorce decree, awarded to Frank Heffron from Naomi Heffron, on the grounds of abandonment.

"But I never received notice of this!" Naomi was dismayed beyond belief, and she could no longer keep away the tears. "And how could I have abandoned him when he was the one who left me back home?"

"I've heard this is common practice out here," Ruth said, placing the document back in the box, her hands shaking. "Men come out here, find a fancy woman or a respectable one with money to settle down with, set divorce proceedings in motion on this pretext, and it's legal, because the wife never came here with her husband. So the court says she has abandoned him." She sat on the bed and looked at Naomi with pity in her eyes. "And of course, it's the other way around. The man gives a fictitious address for the wife, and she never learns of it. She may go through life never hearing from her husband again."

Naomi was shocked. How could Frank have done such a thing to her? He was not a cruel man. She didn't understand, but there it was. And what about Josie?

Ruth Heffron looked down at her hands, which were gripped tightly together. "I had money from my first husband. He died in a cave-in. Only now the money's all gone, pledged to this last silver mine."

She looked at Naomi, and at tiny Josie asleep on the bed. "So, my dear, you are truly divorced. And I am truly married to the man you thought was still married to you."

She hesitated. "I can no longer love Frank, knowing he has done this to you. And he can be so charming . . . but neither can I support myself without him. He has made one bad investment after another with my money. If this new claim doesn't work, he may leave me and do the same thing, move on to greener pastures and richer women." Ruth smiled faintly. "But I shouldn't be worried. Everywhere you dig around Leadville there is silver."

Naomi brightened at what Ruth said. "I can support the two of us if he does leave," she answered. "I'm a school teacher. I heard people talking about the new school here in town. I can apply for a position."

But then she looked down at her sleeping child. "I would have to have someone to look after Josie while I teach. And I could not use my married name — someone might put two and two together. A divorced woman couldn't teach children. And what if Frank saw me on the street?"

"Frank needs to know what he has done, Naomi. He won't turn away his own child; he longs for one. And I will tell him what you have had to do to keep from being penniless. When I get through with him, he won't dare complain about anything. You will always be welcome in my house, and he will just have to get used to having his two wives in the same town. If he does leave, the two of us will make do."

And so it was settled. Ruth found Naomi a decent set of rooms nearby, not an easy thing in this boomtown. Naomi, who knew her teaching craft, impressed the principal of the new school and soon had a job teaching the first grade.

Josie thrived with the care of her two mothers, and Naomi came to love the children who came daily to learn their three R's. Frank did strike it rich, but he never felt rich again at home. When Naomi came to supper, talking animatedly with Ruth of her school day, he would sit and look with bewilderment at the two of them. Only Josie, who became his pride and joy, kept him in Leadville, where he became secretly known among the women of the town as The Man With Two Wives.

Bear Mother

FOUR
Bear Mother

*S*he would take little Grace for a walk in the woods, look for blackberries. Anything would be better than staying in this dim platform tent. It was never warm here unless the sun was shining, and that possible only for a few hours. Even the sun hesitated to shine into this narrow canyon, its depths carved by a sharply rushing river.

Surely even this high in the mountains there would be berries to pick now that it was summer. After all, the bears must find something to eat in this wilderness. The day was still cool, so Renata wrapped her heavy black wool shawl around her. It blended into the black wool of her skirts that had rusted with age since she left the East and civilization.

Skipping ahead of her, in bright calico, young Grace was happy to be out of the drab settlement. Her sweater flew open as she went, but she seemed unaffected by the chill. She swung her metal pail as she looked into the bushes for berries. She exclaimed joyfully when she startled a butterfly, bright and ephemeral, that had been resting on a bush.

The trail climbed along a small creek, and Renata paused to catch her breath. She would never get used to the high altitude, nearly at the treeline, nor did she want to get used to the whole desolate place. All that had been happy in her life, save Ralph and especially Grace, was rooted in the lush green forests and fields and towns that held her family back home. If it had not been for little Grace, Renata would have withered away here. Like her spirits, even the greenery had to struggle to live on the steep mountains.

The gold miners seemed to fade physically just as their dreams faded. They saw more and more worthless dirt in their pans. Little gold, day after day. Ralph had been enthusiastic at first. Now Renata watched him fight to wake up daily, struggle out into the numbing water with pan, pick and shovel.

She could not reach him any more.

Renata and Grace came to a bush laden with berries beside the trickling creek. The little girl laughed and began the task of filling her bucket. Renata stooped to join her, both intent on their job. Most of Grace's berries went into her mouth, making Renata smile at her stained lips. She wondered if Ralph had found any nuggets today.

Ralph spent his days up a bigger stream, panning for elusive treasure. He was entranced with the chase, the lure of riches. Sometimes he found enough sparkling flecks to pay for the day's provisions, and then the feverish light of the chase lit his face. Unevenly and oh so slowly his poke grew, but it was never enough for him to quit.

Renata sighed and put more berries into her half-full bucket. Ralph couldn't see that this was no place for a child. Grace needed other children, a school.

Renata should have listened to Papa. They had all heard tales of failures in the gold fields. It was bad enough that she had to bake bread for the mercantile to bring in a steady income. When she had married a dreamer she had married one of those failures.

Ralph had grown away from her, consumed by his quest. He had always loved the outdoors, as Renata had always sought the warmth of her hearth and her home. When he came home as the sun faded, with his nearly frozen feet and blue fingers, he was so excited. Look here! Look at the size of this nugget! And look here how much today's lot weighs! But she knew from talk in the mercantile that none of the miners had found enough to make much difference at all.

Renata supposed she was a poor wife for a miner. Even though the few other women here also hated what their men did, she could find no solace in their company. They seemed shallow, determined to put on a good face, as futile an attempt as trying to keep their platform tents free from the incessant dirt and mud their men tramped in each night. Those other women — the ones in the saloon tent — were more intriguing. But she couldn't talk to them despite their sometimes wistful looks as she passed by with young Grace. There were few other children, only toddlers and babies.

They'd come to another berry-laden bush. The child rose to reach another branch of blackberries. Renata straightened to ease the crick in her back and looked down over the forested hillside.

Two moving shapes came over a rise, some scrub masking them from time to time. A black bear and her cub.

Thank God not a grizzly.

Renata clamped one hand over Grace's mouth and hugged her tightly with the other arm, her black shawl around them both.

The bears headed toward them, drawn to the same clump of berry bushes where the two stood frozen. The wind was gentle on Renata's tense back, and the mother bear had not smelled them. Dear God! What to do?

The animals came on.

Fear gripped Renata as she realized fully their danger. No! They would not harm Grace! Renata's mind flashed through a montage of retreats, of possibilities, but rejected them all.

Grace trembled in her arms.

This could not be happening. What could she do? This land had fought her every inch of this last winter, and now it wanted her. It wanted her child.

The mother bear stopped to root at something, and Renata stooped quickly to whisper in Grace's ear.

"Don't move until I say so, and then run back along the trail to the camp as fast as you can. Send someone here. Go to the saloon. The bartender will be there. Then go home."

The bear raised her head. Had she heard Renata's frantic whispering? The animal stood up on her hind feet and looked right at the two of them.

"Go!" Renata thrust the child from her, and the berry pail spilled its rich load as the frightened child dropped it. The clatter on the rocky soil startled both of them. Grace's blue sweater caught on a branch, and for a moment Renata thought all was lost. But Grace yanked the garment free, then fled.

The bear roared and dropped to four feet to charge. Her cub was in danger! The cub began to climb a big pine tree.

Renata ran to intercept the bear, keep it from catching Grace. She grabbed a long fallen branch with a pointed end where it had broken from the tree. Maybe she could kill the animal. She was shaking with terror.

She ran until she was between Grace and the bear. She scrambled onto a boulder, spread her black shawl wide, and cried, "NO! YOU WILL NOT HAVE MY CHILD!"

The bear stopped, perhaps astounded by the size of the woman on the boulder with her spread shawl, her skirt flapping and billowing.

"Go back!" Renata bellowed, her voice frantic! "Leave us be! Go!"

The bear would have to kill her first, and she would not die easily.

She gripped the branch, her shawl clenched, one end in each hand, widespread. Her trembling stopped as she focused on what she had to do.

The wind freshened and changed direction. The shawl flapped. The sounds of Grace's flight died. There was only the bear's panting and her own thudding heart.

The cub bleated a thin cry from its perch in the tree, and the mother bear looked back at it. Then she gathered herself, came through the bushes as if they didn't exist. Renata could see the powerful muscles ripple under the rich black fur, the glare in the bear's eyes, tongue lolling over sharp teeth. The animal raced uphill with no effort at all.

Renata leapt down from the boulder, calmer now that Grace was out of harm's way. Her heart still beating fast.

She whipped the shawl from her shoulders and held it with her left hand, fumbled with the heavy branch in her other hand.

Another plaintive sound from the cub.

The bear roared again, then rose on her hind feet. She was only ten feet from Renata, but Renata would not run. The bear's glossy black coat rippled over her strong shoulder muscles.

Renata held her ground. The bear dropped and charged.

Renata flung the heavy shawl. The bear ran full into it, paused to fight off the thing that muffled her sight. Bellowed again. Trampled the shawl.

She was almost upon Renata, who backed up frantically.

No time to think.

With all her strength, Renata thrust the pointed branch full into the bear's open mouth between the long pointed teeth. The shock of the collision threw her backward into the boulder.

Hastily she gathered herself and scuttled away from the black fury. She tried to run, tripped and fell against another rock. Pain lanced through her shoulder. She grabbed another fallen branch, this one more club-like, and scrambled to her feet.

She had aimed fair. The bear was impaled. It fought the branch wedged in its bloody mouth. Dropped down and convulsively fought its death. Frantic pawing did nothing to dislodge it. The branch must have lodged in bone.

The struggles grew weaker and weaker. Then stopped.

Renata could not move. The world turned around her head and she sank down on the cold ground. She had saved Grace. She had saved herself.

She listened to the cub in the tree making mewling sounds, and a pang struck her. One motherless creature, but not hers. Thank God, not Grace.

At last she heard voices, calling, calling. "Missis! Missis, where are you? We're coming! Where are you?"

She found her voice, though it cracked and stuck in her throat. People crashed through the underbrush: the saloon keeper in his apron carrying a rifle, pockets bulging with shells. Several men he had surely rousted from drunken stupors waved guns unsteadily, clothing awry, eyes bleary but determined. Even women from his rooms in their gaudy short dresses. They clutched weapons of empty liquor bottles and looked quite fierce. Renata recognized women from the tents next to her own, brandishing frying pans and butcher knives, their faces alive with concern.

Renata had beaten the land today. She felt the heavy weight of helplessness that had engulfed her for so long slipping off her shoulders. Instead of weakness in the wake of her victory, she felt strong enough for more challenges in this bitter land.

She stood straight and firm, the new branch tight in one hand. It was a good branch, not dry and brittle but somehow alive in her grasp. She would keep it by her. She walked toward the group, and they could see that she was well.

Always Trust Your Burros

FIVE
Always Trust Your Burros

*G*erta Trader had no use for men. She had been sprung out of civilization when her meek and long-suffering husband, Pete Trader, keeled over one morning in church back in Missouri. She never looked back. Now she sat by a campfire in the Colorado wilderness, her horse, Cassandra, nuzzling her from behind, and burned the last of her dresses.

In the ashes of her civilized life, a question arose. She talked with Cassandra about her means of surviving in the wilderness.

"One," she said, stirring the fire, "I could offer myself as a horse-breaker to a hostelry in the town that should be over the next ridge. You know I've always favored animals over people. But that would mean living in a town, and no one would want me to wear pants instead of skirts."

Cassandra shifted her weight and looked wise.

Gerta continued. "Two: I could wander into the mountains and try to stake out a claim, do some gold or silver mining. But that would mean spending all my days underground, away from fresh air and glorious views of the land, or else standing knee deep in freezing water with chilblained hands. I don't think you'd like that life either."

Cassandra tossed her head. Not a good idea.

"Three: I could cook for a bunch of miners, but I don't even need to ask you what you think of that idea, because it's too sorry to think about. You know I'm a rotten cook and am forever burning myself and the food. Good thing you don't have to eat my cooking." Gerta stopped to consider, rubbing the latest burn on her hand. "Maybe my cooking was why Pete died."

Yes, she would have to think about what to do. Right now it was getting dark and Gerta was tired. She scrubbed out her frypan with dried grass (which didn't get quite all the scorched beans off the bottom), and checked Cassandra's hobbles. Then she prepared to roll herself into her blankets. A smile of contentment hovered around her mouth, exposing a broken tooth.

She had no sooner put her head down on her saddle when Cassandra's head went up from her grazing nearby and her ears pricked forward. Someone was coming. Gerta had learned the hard way to think the worst of men when confronted with a lone woman in the wilderness. She tossed aside the blankets, hastily put her gun belt and boots back on, and made sure her rifle was ready at hand. She moved herself and Cassandra back into the shadow of a tree, away from the campfire. All this took less than a minute.

The sounds of many hoofs slowly came closer. Gerta stiffened. She should have put her saddle back on the horse.

A strange sight came over the rise. A string of burros, heavily laden, and on the first one, slumped over, a man. He called from a distance, weakly, "Hello, the campfire. Help. I'm alone. Coming in."

Gerta moved then. The law of the road said she had to go to his help, but she would have anyway. Cassandra wasn't alarmed; this was not a trap. She ran to meet the pack train. "It's ok, mister. I'm coming."

But when she tried to help the man off his burro, he fell onto the ground, stone dead.

Well, that was just dandy. What was she going to do with a string of burros and a dead man? Maybe she was jinxed; Pete had keeled over at her side too.

The burros stood a little impatiently, waiting to be taken to the water they could smell nearby. Gerta left the dead man by the fire and did just that. Animals came first, and the man had no need of her help any more. It was a long procedure, getting all the heavy loads off the fifteen burros and hobbling them in the dark.

She looked through the man's clothes, searching for identification. She found only a list of the supplies the animals carried, and some mine names. From his route to her fire, he must have been headed for the same town she was aiming for.

The next morning Gerta finally got the hang of loading the burros. She put the dead man, who didn't weigh all that much, on the first burro again, wrapped in her canvas ground cloth — what had happened to that burro's pack? Cassandra was happy for the company of all these animals, though she took umbrage when one of them tried to kick Gerta.

⚜

The man's name was Hector Johnson, and he had been the only one willing to take supply trains to some of the higher, less accessible mines in the vicinity. The doctor thought he'd had a heart attack, all right, and the sheriff agreed. Hector had left the town just two days ago. He must have begun to feel so poorly that he turned around and headed back to town. They thanked Gerta for bringing him in, even staked her to a free night in the one hotel, and they put up Cassandra in the livery stable.

Though she felt sorry for poor Hector Johnson, Gerta's heart leapt at the idea of taking his place, though it was a radical idea. She had worked with animals all her life, she told Miles Everett, the livery man who owned the burros. She could do this easily. All he would have to do was show her the way to the camps once and she'd find her way from then on.

He had seen the care she took of Cassandra, and how well she'd repacked the burros in the morning. There was no one else willing to take on this job, because of the hazards of the trail and the isolation of the work. Every man in town was more interested in staking his own mining claim. But a woman? Even a strong-appearing one in men's pants? However, there was no choice at the moment. Everett rode along at the head of the burro train with her the next day.

Everett told her about the various mining claims and things she might have to pack in, about bringing out ore, and maybe even dead men, if they hadn't wanted to be buried at their claims. Otherwise, he wasn't talkative, so Gerta was free to enjoy the scenery, memorize the route, make the acquaintance of the various burros.

"See here," she finally said to Everett the first night. "I don't know what these animals are called, and I need to name them, unless you can tell me what their names are. I can't just say, 'Hey, you fifth mule in the line, get away from that loco weed!' They'll behave better if they have names."

He looked at her, shrugged, said, "Suit yourself. They're just dumb animals, but they seem to be taking to you just fine."

So it was done.

✠

Gerta Trader and her burros became a fixture in the area. After the initial shock of seeing a woman leading Hector Johnson's pack train, the miners were glad to see her whenever she appeared. In fact, her visits added a little spice to their lives. It would take some time to tell her their tales of woe about mining, their other tall tales about life up near the roof of the world. And they were gentlemen when Gerta was around. Her commanding presence helped reinforce that kind of behavior.

Once a snowstorm stranded her at a mine high above the treeline, and she kept her animals sheltered inside the mine tunnel. This winter had been remarkably cold, and more storms were inevitable. She hadn't brought enough supplies to last the miners for any great length of time, so she talked them into following her back down to town. They would have never been able to find the snow-covered trail on their own.

Gerta loved her animals most of all, and she took excellent care of them.

By the time Gerta Trader had twenty-six burros, one for each letter of the alphabet, she had become acquainted with them enough so that their names fit their personalities. Aleph (first letter of the Hebrew alphabet) always led, unless the snow was deep, and then Excalibur, so good at slashing through the drifts, took over. Gerta always kept an eye on little Napoleon, who had a good instinct to take them around dangerous spots. She had to watch out for Brutus, however, who was sly and liked to kick if she wasn't looking.

One day while traversing a steep slope of treacherous shale, two burros lost their balance and began sliding. Moving fast, Gerta, who had been walking, cut them loose from the others and kept the whole string from following them. They both recovered, and were named Yorick and Lazarus. She had been late on her rounds that time, but Gerta wouldn't rush the animals' recovery.

She never tried to make the burros go where they didn't want to go again.

⚜

One day back in town, Gerta woke up to a great commotion outside. Men on horses were milling around in a cloud of dust. She ran outside to find out what was wrong. The assay office safe had been robbed in the night, and a sizeable amount of gold was missing. "Only two men, both masked, and they made off with their loot in a stolen wagon," the sheriff said, "and they came close to shooting Miles Everett. Tied him up in the corral."

He looked at Gerta and cleared his throat. "They took your horse with them, Miz Trader, tied to the back of the wagon with another good horse, and two sturdy horses in the wagon traces, Everett said."

Gerta's heart plummeted and then began to burn. Take Cassandra would they? She would see about that! She set out with the posse on a stout but ugly black gelding. She loved Cassandra, and she was close to tears as she left town at a good trot.

The robbers had headed south. Did they think they could make it all the way to Mexico before someone caught up with them? Gerta fumed and fretted, and kept a close watch on the rough ground for a glimpse of Cassandra's hoof marks. She lagged behind the several trackers and the sheriff with the rest of the posse.

It was getting late and the wagon tracks were hard to follow when Gerta heard gunshots. She kicked her horse and rounded the bend. Cassandra and one of the robbers were gone. The other lay dead by the wagon, shot by the sheriff. Part of the stolen gold was missing. The sheriff thought the two must have split up in the rocks they'd passed a short while ago. No telling where the other guy had gone. It was too dark to go after him now.

In the morning they went back to the rocky area and Gerta finally spotted one of Cassandra's hoofprints. But they had no Indians to help them track and soon lost the trail among the increasingly steep boulders. All Gerta could think about was the hard pace the thief must be setting her poor Cassandra.

Cursing silently, she decided there was nothing to do but go back to town and take out another pack train. The miners needed food. With her burros, Gerta chose a route that might intersect the horse thief if he kept heading south over the high mountains. She rode the black gelding with a grim expression on her weather-beaten face, looking closely through the firs, the ponderosas, the aspen groves.

The pack train was nearly at the tree line when a sudden thunderstorm flashed out. It would be death to go higher in the downpour and constant lightning. She paused with the skittish animals, twenty-six heads down, Gerta looking around frantically for some place safer than this exposed place.

A mighty thunder crash and a man's hoarse scream!

Gerta turned, and the burros' ears pricked up. She tied the gelding to a tree, praying to God the lightning would pass by. She pulled her rifle out of the scabbard and felt her hip holster.

Running back along her trail and down the slope through a grove of stunted pinyon pines, Gerta spotted Cassandra, standing head down. Her reins were held by a man caught under a fallen tree. He must have been trailing her.

The man saw her coming. He had her in the sights of his rifle before she could slither to a stop and take aim at him.

He kept the rifle trained on her. "Get me outta here, woman, or I'll nail you where you stand."

Gerta didn't argue. She dug him out from under the tree. He walked behind her up the slope back to the pack train leading Cassandra, whose saddlebags bulged. Gerta's rifle was now tied behind the saddle and the man wore her holster over his shoulder. One of his legs was bloody. Good, she thought savagely. He limped badly, but he was still deadly.

"Handy thing I was so close to you," he said with a nasty leer. "I was meaning to have me a little fun before I took your donkeys and supplies. Now you can get me over these mountains and into Mexico."

The thunderstorm departed as rapidly as it had come. She refused to speak to him as they turned away from the claim she'd been heading for. Have some fun with her, would he? She would see about that. Once on the trail, he managed to mount Cassandra from a rock. Gerta bit her lip when he hit the horse on her tender nose as she tried to break free. This man would not live to make it to Mexico.

"Make us a bee-line south, bitch," he commanded. That involved terrain Gerta didn't know, so she had to look for game trails big enough for her animals.

She decided she was as strong or stronger than the man was, hurt as he was, and she kept up a punishing pace. She knew just how much she could push the animals. Several times she noticed the man drooping in the saddle, nearly asleep, but he snapped to attention every time he saw her eyes on him.

At night he tied Gerta to a tree, and though she struggled until her wrists were bloody, she couldn't get free. His injured leg kept him from wanting to "have fun" with her.

The next day in mid-afternoon they came around the side of a mountain to find a chasm looming ahead of them. A landslide had covered the game trail she had been following. The burros stopped.

"Get on with it, bitch!" the man demanded with a snarl. "Get them donkeys across that rock field. We got to get outta here before that sheriff has his Injuns on my trail."

"Can't do it, mister. They won't go. You'd have to carry them. Burros know where they can go and where they can't."

"Then I'll shoot a few of them and see if that makes them hurry up." He limped up from the back of the train, glared at her, then took out his pistol and turned around, aiming at Cassius, third in line.

Unfortunately for him, he'd turned his back on Brutus, who kicked him soundly in the middle of the back. He flew over the edge of the narrow trail. His gun went off, and Hamlet, who had been thinking of other things, no doubt, dropped in his tracks.

Gerta watched the man roll screaming down the steep side of the mountain as she ran back to Cassandra and her rifle. She took aim as his body came to rest with a loud "whack" against a big boulder. He didn't move. She waited. Nothing.

She turned to Hamlet. He lay there twitching, braying piteously. She gritted her teeth and put a bullet through the middle of his forehead. "I'm sorry, dear Hamlet," she said, patting his neck.

Then she went to Cassandra, who stood nervously at the end of the line of burros, her reins dragging. Gerta hugged her best friend and burst into tears.

Soon she recovered herself, put Hamlet's pack on the black gelding, turned the pack line on itself with a surprised Moses in the lead behind Cassandra, and started out of the mountains and back to town.

Gerta caressed her beloved horse's neck as she rode, and she thought about this third man who had met his death in her presence. He was the only one who had deserved to die, but all three had changed her life.

Now she had proved she wasn't just a woman alone in the wilderness: she was a successful woman with a useful job and all these friends. Gerta started to sing in her off-key, creaking voice, and the little burros joined in until the hills rang with happy cacophony. "*Mine eyes have seen the glory of the coming of the Lord* . . . "

Cassandra sighed and flicked her ears.

Prospector Canyon

Jonathan F. Schmauder

SIX
Prospector Canyon

*T*ensia kept her attention on the huge iron fry pan to make sure the potatoes didn't burn. Her face was flushed from the heat of the cook stove. The miners ate noisily at the long trestle tables behind her in the big cookhouse, and Seth shuttled quickly back and forth between the stove and the tables, refilling the serving bowls with stew meat and potatoes.

One voice stood out among the rough sounds of rude men. "*Tensia*! What kind of a name is that?" The men laughed. Buck Hanrahan was the instigator of many a mean trick. "*Hortense*! I'll bet that's what it really is, and our little missy cook is probably a whore from down on the prairie! Might try her out myself!"

The raucous laughs were stilled when the boss roared out over them, "Forget about it! You want to lose this cook too? She's a good cook, and too skinny for a good whore. Save your fun for Saturday nights down in Animas Forks."

Tensia's hands shook so hard she spilled hot potatoes on Seth's wrist as he stood holding another serving bowl. She glanced at his face and saw a black expression that frightened her with its intensity, She knew he wasn't angry because of his burned wrist. The men had their fun teasing him too, but he always seemed more upset when they talked this way to her.

The men finally left for the bunkhouse. She and Seth cleaned up the kitchen mess, washing the tin plates, the big cast-iron pans, and the utensils. They rarely talked, he being too shy and she too kind to break into his reserve. He went to dump the slops through the trapdoor into the gulch.

Tensia started to take off her apron, when a change in the air made her turn. Buck Hanrahan was upon her before she could move, whispering filthy things, fumbling with her skirt and her breasts, breathing his rancid breath in her face. Weighted by his body, she fell back against the sink, her mind a red-hot fury. Her flailing hand touched the big butcher knife.

She wrenched the knife upward and under Hanrahan's ribs just as the huge iron fry pan descended on the back of his head.

The man crumpled at her feet, blood spouting over her white apron. Tensia looked at the ashen-faced Seth, who stood with heaving chest, the fry pan dangling to the floor from both his hands.

Tensia was frozen with terror. The men would kill the two of them! Or it would be prison.

She couldn't bear the thought of being locked up, especially after this miserable winter in Picayune Gulch. Where could she go?

Seth threw the pan back on the counter, ran for coats, blankets, snowshoes. He came back and fumbled at Hanrahan's boots. "You'll get nowhere in those shoes of yours," he said. "Wrap your feet in these clean dishtowels and put on the boots. Hurry!"

Yes, she had to flee. She tore off the bloody apron, dunked her hands in the drinking bucket until the water was red and her hands white, dried them on her skirt.

Outside, she stared down, still in shock, as Seth laced her ungainly-booted feet onto showshoes. "Uphill," she said. "I'll go uphill. They'll never think to look in that direction. I'd rather die than be caught. You go to the bunkhouse with hot coffee. They won't know you were involved."

She trudged out into the falling snow, heading left up toward the snow-blocked pass, feet splayed wide to accommodate the big showshoes.

Seth called out, "I'm coming with you. You'll never get through alone."

"No! You musn't! You have your whole life to look forward to." She turned again and hurried on as fast as the ungainly gear would let her.

On and on, her skirts finally picking up enough snow to become heavy as a metal bell on the ankles of the boots. She fell. Someone picked her up. Seth, of course.

They staggered on through the storm, uphill, Tensia's breath coming ragged with the effort at the altitude, her legs burning with pain. She'd heard the pass here was over 13,000 feet. Her lungs cried out, starved. Even the wool blanket clutched over her mouth and nose didn't warm the air enough to keep the cold from slicing into her lungs. The two of them fell again and again, first one and then the other.

When she thought she could go no farther, the snow leveled out, though the wind swept up from the right and made drifts they had to inch around. The snow stopped, and racing clouds scudded above them. Wind blew the snow swirling in graceful whorls. A cold moon looked down and said nothing.

They were at the top of the pass, and to their right was an awful drop into a narrow canyon far below. She and Seth tried to make no noise; an avalanche would be the end of them.

Beyond and curving down the left side of the canyon was a narrow donkey path cut into the wall of the gorge. Clouds built up again, and the moon disappeared. Could the two of them make it down that snow-covered cut in the steep hillside without sliding over the edge?

On they went, until Tensia felt in a trance, on a never-ending journey to oblivion. She couldn't feel her feet, nor her fingers. At least they were headed downhill. No thought of turning back, though the way seemed endless. How long was this path? The snow strengthened with the wind, which howled and shrieked at them. A particularly vicious swirl sent Seth crashing into Tensia and they fell, sliding. He threw his arms around her and dug in his snowshoes to keep them from crashing down to the bottom of the chasm.

They struggled to their feet and locked arms. Together or not at all they would continue.

A light appeared ahead of them, bobbing dimly in the driving snow as if attached to a slowly walking animal. A donkey, maybe a horse. They must have caught up with a prospector edging his own way down off the heights! They tried to hurry but could make their frozen bodies and unwieldy snowshoes go no faster. They called out but he never answered.

On and on, down and down. The road leveled out after a short steep stretch that had them both down face first in the swirling snow. When they got to their feet, the prospector's light made them turn to the right. The snow cleared enough for them to see that if they had slid farther they would have been in a frigid stream laced with snow-covered boulders.

Tensia was numb from her head to her feet. Why didn't the prospector wait for them? Maybe he was drunk.

She realized the dark had given away to a grim gray dawn. They had walked all night. Ahead of them was the dim outline of a building.

A steam whistle blew its harsh wake-up, and the snow dwindled off into a flurry. Seth pointed. "Men! We're at a mine! Must be Animas Forks." He staggered faster, pulling her on with him, until she fell senseless into the white pillow of snow.

Tensia woke up to the exquisite pain of frost-bitten feet and hands being rubbed back to life by a kind-faced woman. She turned her head. Another woman was bending over Seth, who was also on a bed. He stared at her with an intensity that gave way to a weak smile when he saw her move.

She told the story of their flight, but another version. They had left the camp because one of the miners tried to force himself on her, she said, but she had fought him off. She would rather die than submit to him or any other man, she said, and she was not lying about that. Seth had been in the bunkhouse, she told them, and had come outside in time to see her walk by.

They had followed the prospector all the way down. Where was he? She wanted to thank him.

The women looked at each other uneasily. "No prospector up there in this weather," one finally said.

"Ghost of Tam Melville," replied a second.

"Couldn't be Tam," argued a third. "He hated women. His wife left him to become a whore."

"But you heard that tale of how Charlie Flint followed someone back to the camp when a sudden snowstorm turned into a whiteout. Guy disappeared the minute the snow let up, and Charlie could see the town ahead of him."

The women all looked at Tensia speculatively.

Feeling the life come back into her feet with exquisite pain, Tensia grimaced and said, "Whoever he was, he was an angel. We would be frozen up on the pass somewhere if we hadn't seen him. He couldn't hate all women just because his wife was bad, could he?"

The women began to nod at each other. One laughed. "Tam would split his sides, being called an angel!"

Another woman said, "That man who came after you in Picyune Gulch — he wasn't Buck Hanrahan, was he? No wonder you ran. He's got a reputation for meanness as bad as a rattlesnake."

Tensia looked at Seth with new hope. Tam Melville's ghost might stay around Prospector Canyon helping people, but there had been a second angel with her all the way from Picayune Gulch.

Good Friends

SEVEN
Good Friends

*O*ther women, even the church-going wives of honest businessmen, looked on Sophie's beauty with envy when she rode out in her elegant carriage. She was fond of wearing an ostrich plume in her jet-black hair and brilliant diamonds around her neck. Her well-cut gowns, modest enough for the daytime, set off her magnificent figure.

On the night it happened, Sophie had noticed a few more lines in her fine-boned, aristocratic face as she put on her make-up. She turned down the lamps another notch before her evening appointment arrived. She thought of all the money she had saved, but she also thought of how fast it could go and how she would make a living when she was old. She did not want to be a madam, as much as she enjoyed giving men pleasure and receiving it in return. She wanted a change.

Mr. Kydd was ushered in, and there was something about his appearance tonight that gave Sophie pause. He had always given her the impression of being a sleeping rattler, but tonight he was tightly coiled. He paced the room and refused to settle down to the light collation the maid had brought up from the kitchen. He circled the small round candle-lit table, picked up a fruit knife and put it down. He glanced at Sophie from under his dark brows and answered her gentle questions with impatient, short answers.

She was wary, and kept some distance between them.

After a few glasses of wine it all came out: his betrothed back in Virginia had written that she would not come to this godless land in the Colorado mountains, not for all the gold in his mine. If he would not come home, she would marry another.

Kydd became more and more agitated as he told this bad news. He glowered at Sophie. She thought to pull the bell cord for Spade, who was strong enough to manhandle any client in the Old Homestead bordello. But as she glided across the room, her heart racing, Kydd lost all control.

He strode after her and threw her on the pillow-covered bed. Sophie couldn't reach the small derringer she always kept in a hidden pocket at the head of the bed. She fought desperately, but he was upon her, whispering a torrent of promises of what he was going to do to her, to all women, to that faithless bitch back in Virginia. He tore off her peignoir, bruised her breasts with a violent squeeze, then broke her jaw and her nose with his fists. He cut her face with the diamond ring on his hand as he hit her and hit her. The blood filled her eyes and she could feel consciousness leaving her.

Her screams brought Madam and Spade at last, but the damage was done.

♔

When Sophie came out of the laudanum-induced haze she saw Dr. Stevens bending over her. Madam hovered in the background, and young Fanny stood by her with tear-stained face. "I did the best I could, Sophie," the good doctor said. "You just rest now, my dear. We'll see what the damage is in a few days when the swelling goes down."

Madam looked on her with a hard gaze. Sophie had been her biggest moneymaker. "I don't know how you could ever attract another man, Sophie," she said bitterly. "And I won't stand for you setting up another house in this town. Promise me you won't do that and I'll help you any way I can to go somewhere else for a new life."

Sophie couldn't talk, with her jaw bound up. She nodded, and even this small movement made pain lance through her head. She knew this was a business decision on Madam's part. She didn't blame her. Neither did she think she could stand traveling for some time.

Within a short time, Madam had found Sophie a small house on a back street, well away from the cribs that lined Myers Avenue and Poverty Gulch, nowhere near the Old Homestead.

What would Sophie do to keep her money from fading away? What could she do with a damaged face?

She wore a heavy veil and her most sedate black gown and cloak the dark night Spade moved her things in the grocery wagon. He had found her a good bed, a table and chairs, and then he tipped his hat and said good-bye. Spade was a strange person. He had no interest in women at all, not even as friends.

Sophie pulled the shades in the silent house, lit a candle and sat in one of the chairs. She was a survivor and had no time for self-pity. But what could a disfigured woman do in this world?

She heard a whine and a scratching at the door. Her heart fluttered and pounded before she realized the noise was not a human, but more likely a dog.

Ready to slam the door quickly if she was wrong, Sophie cautiously opened it a crack. Dark eyes glittered near the ground, and a medium-sized black dog pushed his nose into the crack, his body quivering all over with cold and with the force of his frantically waving tail.

"I don't need a dog. I have all the problems I can handle, and then some." Sophie's voice was hard to understand, with her jaw immobilized by the bandage around it and over her head.

She started to close the door, but the animal's pathetic eagerness touched her heart, and she reluctantly let it in. The dog's short hair was matted and filled with debris. He smelled. He licked Sophie's hand even while he cringed. That did it.

"You've been beaten, poor thing."

Tears came as she realized the animal and she had much in common. Sophie sat in the chair again and petted her new dog while she cried for the both of them. When it was light, she put heated water in the sink, lifted the dog in, and scrubbed away his filth.

Sophie named the dog Rex, and he became the king of her heart. Weeks passed, and the dog's presence healed Sophie's soul. She went to the mercantile for food in her black dress and cloak and heavy veil, struggling through the snow when winter clapped down on the town. Men pretended not to know her.

No one came to Sophie's house except Dr. Stevens, who tried not to let his pity show. Finally he proclaimed her jaw healed enough to remove the bandage, and she was able to eat more than minced food and broths. By this time her clothing hung loosely, but she did not care. She had not unpacked any of her mirrors, and would not.

A snowstorm came and went on for days. Sophie ran out of food, and she could not bear to look at the hunger in Rex's face. Perhaps she could navigate her way to the mercantile. She could see a faint packed trail down the street in the snow. She put on her heaviest clothing and boots, started to tie a hat around her head with her veil, and went to the door.

A knock made her start. Who could be out in this blizzard? Warily she opened the door to find a snow-covered form carrying a big box.

"I knew you must be out of vittles, ma'am, cause you ain't been to the store since this here storm started. I brung you some supplies."

Sophie's shock gave way to a jolt of warmth — someone had thought of her! But she didn't have her veil lowered, and she turned away. Rex was joyfully alight with welcome, dancing about, his tail a blur of motion. The man must be trustworthy. Sophie steeled herself, then turned around. "Come in. You must be frozen."

"Thankee, ma'am. I am a mite cold." The man stepped in and then looked down, flustered as he saw how much snow he had brought in.

"Never mind the snow, Mr . . . ."

"Green, ma'am. Horace Green. I been helping out at the mercantile, since I sure ain't had no luck in the diggings."

Rex followed the box of groceries to the table. Mr. Green asked for a rag and wiped the floor.

Sophie soon had a pot of coffee going, and she fed Rex. Horace Green talked of the storm, how horses floundered and supplies were short, how fights had broken out in saloons when men couldn't get to their claims. He'd realized he wasn't cut out for the life of a gold miner. Maybe he'd start a mercantile of his own, once he'd saved enough for the enterprise. He didn't stare at Sophie, and he looked kindly on Rex and petted him while he talked. He seemed to be a dam pent up with no one to listen to him. Sophie relaxed.

Horace Green finally stood up after his third cup of coffee. "I'd best be gettin' back to the store, ma'am." He looked at the floor and shuffled his feet. "May I come back with more food when this runs out, and maybe sit with you, ma'am? You're the first woman to listen to my ramblings without looking to see which pocket my poke is in. I'd take it mighty kindly, if I wouldn't be bothering you too much."

Astonished but inordinately pleased, Sophie said yes.

"Well, Rex," she said as she closed the door. "Perhaps we have a friend after all."

The snowstorm stopped. The next night another knock on the door. Sophie's heart lurched — was it Horace Green?

But Rex was furious, and he raced to the door, hackles raised, with a barrage of barking. It wouldn't be Horace Green.

Sophie called out, though Rex thrust himself between her and the door.

"It's Fanny. Open the door, Sophie, I'm freezing."

Sophie decided she couldn't go through life shrinking at every knock on her door. "Hush, Rex, why are you barking at Fanny? She's a friend," she murmured. She opened the door.

Jack Kydd burst in, a wicked grin on his face, obviously drunk again. Sophie had a glimpse of poor Fanny stumbling off down the snowy street. Rex launched himself at the man and fastened his teeth in one leg. Kydd roared with pain. Only Sophie's quick move saved the dog from the slash of the champagne bottle on his head. Instead, the bottle hit her hip, and she gasped. Glass and champagne flew everywhere.

Kydd said, through gritted teeth, "So, my dear, you have a small champion." He grabbed Rex by the scruff of his neck and threw him out the door. Sophie heard a yelp before the door slammed.

"But I'm to be your champion, my dear. Come now, let's put all this behind us. Take off your clothes. I had to pay

Madam a hefty sum for your lost services, or she'd have sent me to the clink. Now I'll take it all back in trade."

Sophie fought hard. He laughed, not feeling her blows, and backed her into the bedroom. "Nothing like a good fight, even from an ugly whore." He spun her around and she crashed into the brass bedstead, her dress ripping as he grabbed it.

On her knees, she slid one hand under her pillow and grabbed the cold, waiting derringer. Kydd began unfastening his trousers. She turned and pulled the trigger. He fell on her, swearing.

Sophie shoved the tiny gun at his chest. The report was muffled this time.

The door crashed open and Horace Green strode in, Rex at his heels still barking furiously.

Horace grabbed the motionless Kydd and threw him aside. He picked Sophie up as if she were a weightless feather pillow. Rex barked and snarled at the silent form. "What will I do?" Sophie wailed. "They'll hang me for murder."

"No they won't, Miss Sophie," Horace said soothingly as he laid her on her bed. He took the gun from her hand. "No matter what you been, no one will put up with a woman being raped. I'll go for Doc Stevens. You got a mighty bad scratch down your back, not to mention that bruise you're sporting on your arm, and your dress tells the rest. You just lay there. Rex will watch over you."

When Dr. Stevens came in with the sheriff, Rex crowded close to her as she sat hugging the remains of her blue dress with the obscene purple splotch to her. He didn't bark.

"You're lucky you have two such good friends, Sophie," said the doctor. "Horace said he heard Rex barking from way up the street and he got here in time to kill that bastard with your gun. Those bitty things do pack a punch up close."

"But I . . . ."

"Now, Sophie, no talking. You're lucky he didn't go for your jaw again. Just take this bit of whisky to dull the pain of those bruises. You'll feel better in the morning."

Sophie glanced at Horace, who looked down at his feet and the snow melting in a puddle.

Two deputies came in after the sheriff and took away Jack Kydd. Horace set to work on the bloody floor.

Sophie hugged Rex as he put his wet paws on her lap and licked her face. She looked at Horace again, with speculation in her eyes, calm now. Mercantile, he'd said? That might be a nice investment. She could always get someone to help him wait on customers, while she looked after the books. She couldn't smile yet, but she knew she would soon.

Converging Tracks

Sheric Fox Schmauder

EIGHT
Converging Tracks

Georgia wiped the perspiration from her mother's forehead and took the blood-flecked handkerchief from her hand. The pale woman lay back on her rumpled pillow, smiling weakly.

"Georgia, my dearest, whatever would I do without you? You have such talent, and instead you spend all your time waiting on me and tending the other children. When I'm better you can draw to your heart's content."

These last words slurred as her eyes closed and she drifted into the sleep that was becoming more prolonged, every day. Georgia worried that some day soon her mother would drift off and never wake up.

The twelve-year-old looked away, tears in her eyes, and checked to see that little Chloe was still happily sitting in her drawer-bed on the floor playing with the rag doll Mama had made for her. Then she washed the blood from the rough handkerchief with cold water.

Mama would never be well. Georgia would have to forget about those art lessons in Denver. Papa had said that the move would come as soon as he hit pay dirt in the little mine he and the others worked. But the seam was elusive, maybe gone. Still Papa set off every morning at daylight for the mine in his work-torn Levi pants, his canvas jacket that never came clean, his tough boots the color of dirt. And every night he came back to the little cabin so tired he could barely stay awake long enough to eat, to talk to Georgia and Sylvan about their day, to rock little Chloe to sleep.

"Tobias," Georgia would hear her mother whisper when he turned out the lamp, "Hold me close. I am so cold I fear I will never be warm again." Georgia would cry silently then, in her own bed with Sylvan cuddled up to her. The little cabin was warm, and her mother should not be cold in her bed heaped high with quilts.

Georgia worked too, doing more and more of the tasks that Mama had done when she had been better. Sylvan was no help — he was only five, but at least he was a good boy, though far too interested in finding his own gold. He brought in a new collection of pebbles every day from the holes he dug behind the tiny house. Every night he asked, "Is this gold, Papa? What does that streak mean? What kind of rock is this?"

Georgia made him keep his collection under the back stoop. No room in here for anything but the two beds, Chloe's drawer-bed, the table and chairs, the stove and the sink. She kept her drawing pad, pencils and eraser under the bed she shared with Sylvan, along with her shoes when it was warm, and her two treasured books, *Little Women*, and the big one with pictures of famous paintings. Papa had found that book by the side of the road where some traveler with an overloaded wagon had left it, carefully wrapped in oiled canvas.

One morning Georgia woke to the sound of Papa crying. She knew what had happened.

At the funeral, Georgia looked more plain than ever, her stocky figure dressed in the new black dress Papa had bought for her. She had hemmed it to fit herself, since it had been made for a full-grown woman and was too long. Her flyaway mouse-brown hair struggled from under the bonnet Mrs. Hall, next door, had given her. Mama was in a plain pine box. There wasn't enough money for a fancy coffin.

When Georgia looked at the body, it wasn't really her Mama any more. Mama had come to Georgia in her sleep last night and said she was all right now. Georgia was to follow her dream, but Mama warned that it might take some time.

Summer came. Georgia cared for little Chloe, who cried because Mama wasn't there to hug her. Sylvan had turned into a silent child, even quieter than Papa. Georgia thought it would be good if Sylvan could go to school in September, but since he was only five there was little chance of that. Georgia herself wouldn't be going back. She couldn't leave Chloe and Sylvan home alone. And who would do the housework if she went back to school?

Instead she drew pictures of her mother. She drew pictures of happier times, like the picnic last summer in the meadow, surrounded by wild flowers. Her only free time was when Chloe slept and Sylvan looked for rocks, after she had finished the dishes and swept the floor and washed clothes.

One Sunday Papa put on his suit, buttoned his white shirt to his neck and tied his tie. He said, "I am going out to bring back a new mother for you children. She's a good woman and will take care of you while I work. Her name is Rose."

Rose? What kind of a name was Rose? Shouldn't she be Miss Somebody, or Mrs. Widow Lady?

Papa's new wife came into the little house where the three children were waiting quietly in their good clothing to welcome her. Papa looked happy, but worried too, when he looked at Georgia. He set down Rose's small trunk and said, "Children, this is your new mother. Show your manners, now, and welcome her." Then he waited, and the smile on Rose's face seemed pasted on. Her hair was a reddish brown, and it was done up in a braid around her head. Her eyes were a brown darker than her hair. There were little lines around her eyes. Georgia thought no one but herself might have noticed that detail.

Georgia knew Chloe and Sylvan needed a mother, so she would not say anything for now. It had dawned on her that the woman must have come from one of the saloons. Her wedding dress was too lacy and too low-cut, though she had placed a silk kerchief in the neck to hide her bosoms. The dress was bright blue with black trim.

Georgia realized Rose was a Scarlet Daughter of Prosperity. She remembered Mama mentioning that word one day as they passed a saloon on the way to the mercantile.

How could Papa do this to them!

Georgia could tell that Rose knew what she was thinking, because the woman just nodded at her and didn't try to hug her or even take her hand. Instead, she hesitated, pain in her eyes.

Turning, she picked up Chloe and made friends with her, and let the child show her the rag doll Mama had made for her. Sylvan had brought in the best of his rock collection and spread it out on the table to show his new mother. Rose let him tell her about each stone and made him feel important. She knew the way to the children's hearts, but not to Georgia's.

Now Georgia knew for sure she would never get to Denver and become an artist. Papa would spend his money on Rose when he struck pay dirt in the mine. Rose would want to stay here with Papa and the mine, not go away to Denver. Rose would think art lessons were a waste of money. She would think Georgia should learn practical things, like cooking and sewing. Georgia hated to sew. Georgia decided that day she knew all about Rose, and what she knew wasn't good. She hated Rose.

♛

At least Rose was a better cook than Mama had been. Sylvan liked her because she thought his rock collection was beautiful and important. He would make a fine miner, Rose told him. Chloe began talking. The first time she called Rose "Mama," Georgia had to turn away to hide the tears.

She went for a walk, taking her sketchbook. She stopped and perched on a rock. Taking out a pencil, she started to draw her own Mama. Dismayed, she had to stop when she couldn't remember just what Mama's ears had looked like.

Georgia slammed the sketchbook closed and jumped up. Fine daughter she was, if she couldn't remember her own mother's ears. Seething because of her bad memory, she walked heavily down to the new train station.

Next week the first train would arrive in Silverton from Durango. Hundreds of men, Chinese and American, had been blasting out the granite of the Animas Forks River Canyon for months, foot by foot, to make the roadbed. Papa had brought granite from the blasting to Sylvan, who became a font of knowledge about the construction. Georgia had never seen a train, but she knew about them. She had been planning to go to Denver on this train as soon as she was old enough to go to art school.

She drew the station and the tracks receding in the distance, interested in the perspective. If she could see far enough, would they disappear into one thin line? And then what would happen to them? Silverton offered no long views; it was hemmed in by mountains. What did a prairie or a desert really look like, not the ones in books? How far could you see on a flat desert? Georgia would have to wait six long years to find out, when she would be eighteen. And maybe not even then. Would Papa ever discover his gold seam?

Georgia stopped drawing and sat on the edge of the wooden platform looking down the tracks with eyes unfocused. She would never go anywhere. She would live with a prostitute until she was eighteen, and the women in the store would still whisper about her behind their hands, like they did now. Papa would keep saying, "Rose is a good woman."

Did Papa know that Rose still drank? Georgia was sure he didn't. She was sure Rose had lied and told him that she wouldn't drink anymore. She tried to hide it from Georgia but couldn't. Other than that, Rose was nice, Georgia had to admit. She had made over one of her fine lawn petticoats for Georgia to wear, and she had bought some soft green wool and made her a winter dress. Georgia hoped she would grow out of it before she had to wear it in the winter. She already had another winter dress that she could let out herself to wear.

The next weekend the whole town went to the new station to welcome the first train to Silverton. Georgia carried her sketchbook and a pencil. The day was hot, and the Scarlet Daughters had fancy parasols to keep the sun off their pale skin. The other women wore bonnets or carried black parasols. A group of Ute Indians stood far away from the tracks, interested but wary. This had been their country before the whites came and built their mines and their towns. Now here was one more white invention to bring strangers into their land.

Everyone heard the train before they saw it. It sounded like all the ghosts in the cemetery wailing to come out of their graves. It echoed in the river gorge, and a curl of puffing smoke rose above the canyon. Georgia was thunderstruck by the tones, the variation as the engineer changed the sound to one of welcome. It seemed to say "Here I come, look at me, I'm the Denver & Rio Grande Railroad train and I come from the world and I bring the world to you, Silverton; to you, Georgia."

Her heart beat faster than ever as the monster came straight at her. She was so shocked that the whistle had known who she was that she forgot to sketch. The crowd waved and cheered and held flags aloft. The big black engine's huge smokestack, so like a funnel, chuffed and snorted, while the headlight shined a fierce eye down the track that grew wider as the train thundered forward. It slowed, hissing out steam. The massive train made Georgia want to cry for her lost dream.

When it was upon them, Papa had to keep a firm grip on Sylvan's hand to keep him from trying to get closer to this behemoth, this black iron monster spurting steam and smoke and calling out to them all. Chloe, in Rose's arms, cried at the noise of the beast and hid her face on Rose's ample bosom.

That broke the spell Georgia had been under, and she began to sketch furiously, standing away from Rose. On the page, the monster grew and Georgia realized she hadn't left room for the cars behind the engine. She forgot everyone as she flipped pages and drew and drew. She sketched the yellow boxcars, the caboose, the passenger cars with all kinds of people alighting from them. She drew the people themselves, the well-dressed women and men, and those who were obviously miners coming to get in on the gold and silver strikes that had been found here.

That night Georgia fell asleep full of the whirlwind of memories about the day, the people, the train.

♔

The summer passed. The train came regularly, and Georgia made excuses to go to the station and draw it again and again until she knew the workings of the great wheels and the pistons that drove them. She drew the conductors and the engineers. They glanced at her, but she was plain and their looks slid over her. She felt this was as close as she would ever get to Denver, watching the train that had wound through Alamosa to Durango and then here.

Papa made her go to school in the fall, which was fine with Georgia because then she didn't have to be in the same place as Rose. Rose was gentle and never punished Georgia for behavior that bordered on rudeness. Georgia was careful not to go too far. When Papa was home she avoided Rose as much as possible. Rose had given away all of her fancy dresses to her old friends, and she wore quiet clothing now. But still she drank, though she managed to be sensible by the time Papa came home for supper.

♛

The winter that Georgia was fourteen the snow didn't stop falling until the train couldn't get to Silverton. The drifts and avalanches were eighty-five feet high on the tracks! Men from Silverton began digging out the tracks, and the telegraph said men were digging from Durango at the other end.

The snow was the least of Silverton's problems. Just before the snow had begun falling, diphtheria came to town. Soon it was raging from house to house. Rose scrubbed the floor and the walls and the table. She forbade Tobias and the children from coming inside with their shoes on. She fought the disease to no avail. Little Chloe came down with it.

Georgia went through the days with a weight in her stomach that wouldn't let her eat. Rose was frantic, and she stopped drinking. She kept Sylvan and Georgia away from the little girl so they should not catch it. The doctor came but could do nothing; the child was too weak.

Tobias stayed home the day his tiny three-year-old died. She couldn't even be buried beside her mother because of the snow and the frozen ground, but she slept in an unheated room at the undertaker's in a little coffin lined with pink silk. When Georgia found out the silk was from one of Rose's old prostitute gowns she was overtaken by a silent hatred, but unable to do a thing. She stopped looking at Rose and never answered unless Papa was there. Rose started drinking again.

Sylvan's seventh birthday was not much of a celebration. Little food was left in town and nothing for a birthday cake. Papa brought Sylvan his own little lump of gold and the announcement that he'd found the vein again. The family was saved. Rose made the birthday boy a special stack of pancakes topped with the last of the watered-down syrup, though without eggs the pancakes were dry. Georgia gave him one of her small sketches of Mama. At first he didn't know who it was, and Georgia had to bite her lip hard to keep from crying.

Papa began to spend more time in the mine, and Rose began to drink even more. The townsmen were still trying to dig out the tracks. Silverton had been isolated more than two months.

Georgia and Sylvan were just out of school on the afternoon the first train from Durango managed to get through the gorge. It had been seventy-three days since the line was closed. Georgia heard the whistle sounding very low and pleased, not as loud and rambunctious as one might expect after such a long absence. Loud noises might start new avalanches. Her heart answered that lonesome call. She felt keenly her longing to be away from this place of sadness and loss.

All of a sudden a competing whistle blew, a frantic call.

A mine disaster.

By the time the two children were in sight of their house at the far end of town, they saw men clustered at the door. Georgia began to run, leaving Sylvan on his own calling for her to wait.

Papa had been buried in a cave-in. They had tried to get to him but had to leave before they were all caught.

Rose sat in a chair, white and still. Georgia barely made it to the bed before her own legs gave out. Sylvan ran in, scattering snow everywhere. He stopped talking again after that.

What would they do? No more Papa between Georgia and Rose. After the funeral service at the undertaker's, where Papa waited with Chloe to be buried beside Mama in the spring, his partners came to Rose. They offered to buy out Tobias Eastwood's share in the mine. That was worth something now that they had found the vein again. Rose, Georgia and Sylvan would not be destitute.

At home, Georgia sat on the bed looking into space, while Sylvan played with his rocks, pretending they were in a mine under the bed. Rose, still in her black dress, sat on a kitchen chair and faced Georgia.

"I know you still think I am a wicked woman, Georgia, but I loved your father dearly. He took me from a life of hell. I know you hated what I had done to stay alive. I know you wouldn't have believed me before, but now you must.

"I was brought to this land by a charming man who promised to marry me. He left me high and dry in the hotel in the middle of the night. I've never heard from him, nor do I want to."

Georgia looked at her. "I could understand doing something you didn't want to do, but why prostitution? That's disgusting!"

"Georgia, I could not get another job. Too many other women were looking for decent work in a town like this. They still are.

"And then the liquor caught me," Rose continued, looking down and twisting her handkerchief, "and I could not get free. Sure, I told Tobias, that good man, that I had licked it, but I lied, wanting so badly to be his wife and out of that place.

"Now I need your help, Georgia, I need you to stop hating me. We need each other. I swear on this Bible that once you help me stop the drinking I will take you to Denver. You will be the artist your father told me you should be. He showed me your astonishing sketches, my dear Georgia; he was a loving and proud father, and he truly meant to take you away from here when there was enough gold to do so."

With a beseeching look, Rose asked, "Will you help me, and help yourself get to Denver?"

Georgia stared with her mouth open, hope rising unbidden in her breast. Could Rose really do this? Tears spilled down Georgia's face and onto her black dress. She willed herself to be hard, to be skeptical, but she failed. Georgia knew the grip of alcohol. She had seen men lying in the gutter, freezing to death, raving, vomiting.

She answered, and her voice was firm. "I will help you, Rose. But if you fail, I will leave you here and take Sylvan with me to Denver. I know how to cope. I will wash clothes and clean for people."

The next months were the fourth hell of Georgia's young life. But her inner fire to be an artist burned as hot as did Rose's need to be free of drink and away from this place that knew her past. And to have Georgia's respect. Sometimes Rose made Georgia tie her to the bed for the night, when the longing for drink was so strong she didn't think she could last until morning. Sometimes she shook and was almost incoherent, but Georgia sat by her and wiped her face and piled on blankets and argued with the demon.

Sylvan sat silently on his bed, white-faced, reassured by both Georgia and Rose that Rose wouldn't harm him when the more violent attacks came, that she was sick and Georgia was helping her get over her sickness.

He knew about sickness, and he was afraid Rose would die. Mama and Chloe and Papa had died.

One day Georgia sat with Sylvan and Rose on the Denver & Rio Grande train and listened to the joyous whistle and felt the lurch of the car jolting her out of her old lost life. They came out of the Animas River Gorge, and there was the wide vista just as she had dreamed of for so long. The tracks kept going and going. Rose reached over and took Georgia's hand, and they both smiled.

This Morning I
Buried My Life

NINE
This Morning I Buried My Life

May 1, 1890

This morning we buried our darling Sarah Jane. At last she is free of the wind that never stops blowing on the prairie, where uprooted tumbleweeds flee helter-skelter. Those ghost bushes are mere skeletons of once firmly rooted plants with green leaves and little spring flowers. Just as my dear little three-year-old was once securely rooted in this world and in our hearts.

I falter when I think that in due time her precious body in the white batiste dress will shrink to mere bones; her blonde curls will fall from her scalp and lie scattered on the satin pillow and the blanket I made for her from my wedding dress.

This afternoon I washed all of the crockery in this small house (not my home; never say "home," though I have left my Sarah Jane under its unforgiving ground). The wind was rising as I washed the white dishes with the delicate blue flowers that she loved. She loved to trace their outlines with her little finger, its tiny nail so perfect and pink.

I washed the brown crockery with the fine gold rim around the edges. I washed what is left of the cups that Karl drinks his coffee from and then breaks in his absent-minded way, missing the saucer and the whole table sometimes, as he reads those ever-lasting books of his. He was in the front room while I washed my blue platter with the fluted edges, reading, reading, his eyes devouring life somewhere else from behind his round glasses.

This morning I buried my life, my blue-eyed Sarah Jane. Her eyes are closed now.

Tomorrow Karl will go back to his newspaper office and write more lies about the beauty and the promise of this land. He wants more people to come here, as his vision is of the future, not of the now. People who pass by this cluster of buildings where the paint is sand-blasted off by the west wind will buy his newspapers and wonder at the difference between what they see and what they read. He will send copies of his newspaper back East on the train that brings us all out once a day to the depot looking for news to arrive from "back home."

Sarah Jane won't be on that train that she laughed to see, screaming with delight at the moaning whistle, clapping her little hands at the melodious "All aboooaard!" of the conductors. Is there a train where she is, so that she can run laughing after it, and ride back to the green groves of my own childhood that she loved to hear of?

After I washed my dishes I pulled down the shades to shut out the cold wind, but I couldn't stop it from coming through the cracks. I took down my fine lace curtains and washed them too, then fastened them on the curtain stretchers in front of the cast-iron cook stove to dry. I went to wash all of our clothing, but when I came to the bureau that held Sarah Jane's clothes, I couldn't open the drawers. I sat in the rocking chair and began to listen to the wind instead.

♔

September 22, 1894

Today we buried our baby Stephen James. We placed him carefully next to his sister Sarah Jane, in the dark ground of the windswept prairie. We will give him a matching tombstone, a smaller arrow pointing up to the washed-out blue sky. And, some say, to heaven.

My baby was only five months and eleven days old. I had no milk to coax him to live, no milk of human kindness, no milk and honey, no nourishment left after four years of mourning my darling Sarah Jane. Karl said I starved the baby, that I fed him dust.

But Karl knows that I must have my one room open to the winds of the prairie, my one room with my rocking chair and my Sarah Jane's dresser. She talks to me on the wind, and if I close the windows she won't be able to get in. I might have missed her if I left the room to feed her baby brother. He didn't mind the sand and fine dirt that piles along the walls and in the corners. I wrapped him in the fine satin of the rest of my wedding dress as I held him in my arms those blessed hours each day. He drank hungrily from my eyes as his sister Sarah Jane whispered in my ears of her home among glades of tall white aspens.

Sarah Jane stays near to me on the mountainside that I can see in the distance. She needs her mamma. Karl has taken me to the mountains in the buggy, but I can never find her, though she laughs and leads me on among the tall waving trees. He will never let me go long enough to find her, but drags me back to the buggy. He is gentle when he ties me to the seat with soft cords of linen, and I never feel them.

Karl tells me he still writes to bring more people to our land, and I think there are more houses around this one. He has planted trees around our own house. The wind slants them toward the east, and they grow crooked, pointing to the mountain where my sweet Sarah Jane lives. Baby Stephen James has gone to live with her, and she will care for him.

I will wash my broken lace curtains today, and fit them on their stretchers, and put them in front of my open windows to dry. The threads of lace will catch the dreams of my lost children, and they will come home on the wings of the dust that gathers in the corners of my room. I rock in my chair with arms open, ready to feed my children again. Already another heart beats under my own.

Recipe for Life

TEN
Recipe for Life

*J*essica thought she would not have a drop of liquid left within her after Harry's funeral. She had cried when the shock of his death in the mine cave-in came crashing through her carefully boarded-up emotions. She had cried when she prepared his poor broken body for his grave. She had cried when she knew for sure that she was all alone with young Catherine in these forbidding Colorado mountains.

Now the other wives and the miners had left the cemetery. The wooden plank stuck in the pile of muddy dirt was all that showed of her loving, rollicking husband of fifteen years. "Harry Croft," the plank read in rough black painted letters; "Born January 27, 1849, Truro, Cornwall, England. Died March 19, 1890. Aged 41. R. I. P."

Jessica took Catherine's arm and guided her back across the rocky slope to their platform tent. Even at twelve, Catherine was nearly as tall as her mother. The girl slumped down on her cot and stared listlessly at nothing. Jessica looked at her. Such a terrible grieving for a child, as deep as her own or more, she thought. But right now Jessica had no strength to do anything at all except try to wall off her own grief.

She began doing what she did whenever there was a crisis. She would cook, but she had no idea what. Cooking always let her put things in perspective. Perhaps it would bring the same insight about death, and her future. She took off her one good dress, which was luckily black as befitted a widow, and placed her one hat back in its tattered hatbox. She put on her old faded wool dress, once bright blue, and tied on her permanently stained apron.

Jessica piled wood in the small stove that was all they had for heat and for cooking. The neighbors had been good about filling the woodbin before the funeral. On the table she set out her mixing bowl and began piling in ingredients. Not much left to cook; she would surely think of something else by the time the mixing was done.

People had left gifts of food while Jessica prepared Harry's body for the coffin. There was still squirrel stew for their supper. Perhaps Catherine would reclaim her interest in the world if she had something sweet after lunch. They had had no breakfast.

Into the yellow bowl with the blue band went two thirds cup of butter, which left a tad more to put on the bread still wrapped in a dishtowel. She only had a cup of sugar left, chunky and hard, instead of the cup and a half she needed. It would have to do. She pounded violently on the lumps with the handle of her mixing spoon until they gave up and splintered into grains. She mixed the sugar with the butter. Three cups of flour, though that left precious little for anything else. Then she went to her treasure trove of hidden things and brought out a tin, filled with nearly a whole cup of raisins that she had been hoarding for a rainy day.

Today it was raining in more ways than one. Jessica looked at Catherine, still sitting on her cot, though she'd drawn a blanket close around her body.

Rest In Peace indeed. Harry, bless his soul, had never stopped laughing and telling jokes long enough to count his cash. He had loaned money and gold dust to anyone who bought him a beer and called him friend. "Gave" money and gold dust was more like it; hardly any of that carefully recorded outflow had turned to inflow. Jessica had done the recording. Jessica had done the cooking and the cleaning and the penny-pinching and the child-bearing. She never minded, since Harry had brought the laughter, the light, the happiness to her life.

Three precious eggs, gift of Mr. Grant, the mercantile man. Into the batter they went, and Jessica tried not to flinch as she spent them all on one cake. A scant teaspoon of cream of tartar — she thought she might skimp on that — but the good measure of a half-teaspoon saleratus.

Now the laughter was gone and Jessica was faced with making her own way. Never would she find the money to go back to

Cornwall, and never would she want to go there. This new land of the Rocky Mountains had been their exciting gamble.

And they both had lost.

The oven felt hot enough. Into the flat baking pan went the batter.

"Do you want to lick the bowl, Catherine?" The child had always loved this treat. No answer. Jessica took the mixing bowl and spoon and put it not too gently in her daughter's lap. Startled, the large brown eyes looked up at her and tears finally spilled over.

The work-worn woman of indiscriminate age with signs of gray in her dark hair and the girl on the verge of womanhood sat together and cried, holding each other fast.

"We will be all right, lass," Jessica promised. "We will make our own way. We Croft women have always been strong, and this land of America pours more strength into those who will fight for it. We are fighters, are we not?"

Catherine looked at her defiantly. "I don't want to fight. I want to have pretty dresses and go to parties and see more than these ugly miners and the painted women that walk out of the saloon. I want to go places and see other things. Now. Da is dead, and now we can leave. Let's pack and go to Denver, at least."

"We can't do that, child. We have no money for our passage anywhere. Your Da gave it all away. But you are tough and so am I. We will find a way."

Catherine looked down at the batter in the big heavy mixing bowl, which had somehow survived the torrents of tears. She put in one finger and gave an experimental lick. "Sugar! What are you making?"

"Surprise. You can already smell it, can't you? What else should we make?"

"But I thought we already were low on supplies when . . . before . . . "

"Yes, we were. But we will blow the whole damn lot today. We will celebrate your Da's life as he would want us to celebrate his life, not his death. Tomorrow we will think of something else."

Catherine smiled at last. It was working! Jessica hoped her sigh of relief wasn't as loud as it felt.

"We have lots of rice. What shall we put in it to make it more appetizing?"

Soon the smell of spiced rice mixed with the tempting smell of the raising cake. "How about some soup, for our first course?" suggested Jessica.

"Soup, by all means!" Catherine sounded almost gay. She went to the crate where the canned goods were kept. "Tomatoes? We have one can left. And tinned milk. Cream of tomato soup?"

"Yes, good idea, but we will fancy it up and call it a mock bisque soup, like I read once on a menu when we were traveling through the civilized part of these United States."

Jessica decided now that her past life was dead she must think in new terms. Civilization would be her watchword. She would no longer look away from the primitive conditions of this hovel. She would have to do something about that without spending a penny, to bring Catherine along in her recovery, and give her a proper life.

They opened the cans and made room for the big soup pot next to the rice that was still boiling. Jessica stole a little butter from her dwindling supply, saving some for the rice (too bad — none left to put on bread for breakfast tomorrow). Salt and pepper. A pinch of saleratus to keep away the sharp taste of the tomatoes.

Catherine washed the flour off the table and brought out their tin plates and some cutlery. Jessica saw her hesitate and put back the third plate; she held her breath, but the girl passed this new crisis with only a small hesitation. Jessica took the raisin cake out of the oven and set it on a cloth in the middle of the table.

"Raisin cake! Where did you get the raisins, Ma?" Catherine took in a deep breath of the glorious aroma.

"My secret, but don't look for any more." She started to lift the pot of squirrel stew onto the stove to heat up while they ate their tomato — no, their mock bisque soup — when a rapping on the wooden side of their tent stopped her.

"It's me, Miz Croft, Hamish Carter."

Jessica raised the tent flap. "Come in, Mr. Carter." Then her eyes looked over the bearded miner, who stood with his battered hat in hand. Several other miners stood beyond him in a line. "What on earth are you all standing out here for?" She stepped out on the step and dropped the flap to keep the heat inside.

"Well, Miz Croft," said Carter somewhat apologetically, "Your man always bragged so about your cooking that we all sat there in the mine while he ate, drooling, if I may use the word, ma'am. Now today after the funeral we was all walking by now and then and we smelled something mighty good coming out of your home."

He looked back at the men behind him, and was prodded and encouraged to continue his recital. With an obvious effort (Hamish Carter had never been known to speak more than three words at once), he went on in a great rush of words. "We was wondering, ma'am, and we don't mean no disrespect to you in your hour of grief, but we was wondering if you might have some of that good-smelling food to spare and could we pay you like, either coins or dust, to maybe cook for us now and then because you see, ma'am, we none of us can cook worth a durn."

Astonished, Jessica stood open-mouthed. Then her mind clicked into action.

"Yes, Mr. Carter, I might manage to do that. But you must understand that I have no utensils for you to eat with and I have nearly exhausted my larder with what I have cooked up tonight. Yes, I guess I could accept payment for my cooking, to replenish my supplies, of course."

At that the several men each whipped out a tin plate and eating utensils that had been hidden under coats, and they nodded at her and at each other with smiles growing on their unshaven faces.

Jessica turned and started to go back inside, then turned again. "But gentlemen, you must understand that I have a young impressionable girl and I will have no rough talk nor behavior, and I will have you be clean when you arrive."

They nodded vigorously and waved relatively clean hands at her and murmured, "Yes, ma'am, of course, ma'am."

Catherine looked up with astonishment at the parade of men as she sat at the table.

The little tent cabin quickly filled to capacity, and the men had to sit on the beds. Their silence and serious attention to their meals was great praise indeed.

And so it came to be that the Widow Croft began to cook for the miners. Mr. Grant saw the advantage to his mercantile business and soon put up another tent on a platform closer to his store, taking in payment a small tightly-negotiated amount for rent. Jessica knew her figures, and she knew to be firm and honest. Mr. Grant could see the determination and intelligence in her eyes, and his respect for her grew.

A growing number of men sat on benches at a long, rough-hewn table and grew contented with Jessica's cooking and Catherine's silent but skillful serving. They washed their own plates and utensils at a convenient tub filled with soapy water behind the mess tent and brought them back each meal.

Jessica was in her glory and Catherine thrived under the new regime. She knew they were saving for their escape from this dreadful, dreary place, and she worked with a will. She never spoke to the miners she served except in the line of business, and she was too young to gather unwanted advances. Jessica hired a man with an injured leg who could no longer work in the mines, and he stirred pots and peeled potatoes under her stern and watchful eye. She herself looked at the supplies Mr. Grant sold her, sifting out the flour weevils, refusing to pay for moldy butter, sniffing carefully at the great hunks of meat to be sure they were still edible.

Her beans were redolent of molasses, her potatoes smothered in smooth gravy, her vegetables cooked just right and flavored with butter and salt. Her roasts and steaks came out tender, and even the scrawny chickens she was forced buy because there were no others were flavored with just the right amount of spices and juices to make them delectable. To be sure, her desserts were heavenly: jelly roll cake, one-egg cake, cider cake. Even her dried fruit pies were delicious, although as the summer wore on she was able to replace the dried fruit with fresh fruits that grew lower in the mountains.

Mr. Grant took a great personal interest in the Widow Croft, and to hear him talk, her success was all his doing. But the men knew that without her magic touch Grant would be back where he was before: a grocer who charged too much for his supplies and was sour to boot.

One early evening after supper, Mr. Grant took matters in his own hands. He too enjoyed Jessica's meals, and he didn't even argue at her prices. Early on he had tried unsuccessfully to negotiate a discount, because of his "liberal" terms on her rental of the mess tent.

Jessica had just removed her new apron and tucked stray hair back into her bun, while Catherine collected the salt and pepper shakers on a tray. Jessica watched as the girl brought them into the kitchen to be covered with a dishtowel against small critters in the night. Then Catherine emptied the sugar bowls into the canister and took off her own bright red calico apron.

When Mr. Grant entered the kitchen by the back door, something in his manner alerted Jessica. "Go on home, Catherine," she said absently. "I'll be along directly. No doubt Mr. Grant wants to talk about the sheep he sold me that was close to being off. Another day and it would have been smelling quite high."

Catherine went out of the tent without another thought, and she didn't see the surprise in Mr. Grant's face. "That sheep was as fresh as could be, Mrs. Croft, and you know it."

"Perhaps I do, Mr. Grant. But I don't want you getting lazy in your selection of merchandise, and I'm reminding you that I keep a sharp eye on my supplies. I have a reputation to uphold."

Mr. Grant, flustered by her direct look and her reminder that he was not the superior partner of this enterprise that he wanted to be, changed tactics. "Perhaps we might walk along the stream before it becomes too dark to enjoy the flowers on the bank."

Jessica's heart began to beat a strange new pattern. What in the world . . . ? Did this man mean to begin what she thought he was planning? She wrapped her shawl around her shoulders against the coolness of the high mountain dusk, wordlessly turned from him and walked out the door, knowing he would follow.

It was nearly dark when she reached her own tent, and Catherine was in bed, almost asleep.

"Where have you been, Ma? I was going to look for you but I was too tired."

"Mr. Grant has asked me to marry him, Catherine. It would mean all our struggles are over. He makes a good living with the mercantile. We can continue our cooking business, but we would have no fear of being cast adrift if the mines fail and the men leave. He isn't a jolly man, like your Da was. But he seems a good man. He does drive a hard bargain in his business dealings. He would take care of you if anything happened to me. I worry about you being all alone in the world, my love."

Catherine sat bolt upright, her unbraided golden hair spilling over her face. "What about Denver?"

Jessica hadn't forgotten about all of that, and her wish to give Catherine more of the world than there was to see in this mining camp. But did marriage to Mr. Grant have to mean the end of all that? And what would it mean in other ways?

"I have not given my consent. I said I would think about it."

In the next days, it appeared that Mr. Grant had taken her hesitation to mean acceptance. He said nothing, but his air became more proprietary. He came into the mess tent more often, and he began to give instructions to Catherine, who was quite capable of carrying on her work without them. She became silent again, and stopped smiling.

Jessica and Catherine did not speak of the pending issue, but Jessica watched from the kitchen. She saw that the miners who so enjoyed her cooking began to behave more deferentially to Mr. Grant, and she saw Catherine's new stiffness. She didn't like much of anything she saw.

Still, the wish for security was strong in Jessica. Anything could happen to a woman out here in the wilderness. She could take sick, die of pneumonia, burn herself badly in the kitchen. What if she died? What would happen to Catherine then? Just last week the stove had nearly overheated before she roused herself from her new abstraction. The tent could have caught on fire.

Jessica decided she had to clear the air with Catherine, who had taken to turning away from her and burying her head in a book in her off hours. She sat across the table in their tent from Catherine and went over all the arguments she had for marrying Mr. Grant (she would of course have to start calling him "George" in private), ticking off the security issues one by one. She exaggerated the dreadful things that could happen to her, things that would leave Catherine an orphan at the defenseless age of twelve. Then she was silent. Time became slow and thick. Catherine kept her eyes down, refusing to look at her mother.

At last Catherine stood up, pushing her chair back angrily. She went to her little trunk, where she kept her schoolbooks, and pulled out a Denver newspaper.

With sharp movements that resulted in a tear across one page, she opened the paper. Appalled, Jessica looked down on an engraving of a two-headed calf. "Is this what you want to be, Ma? Something like this second head, unable to live on your own? Do you want to be Mr. Grant's wife, let him do your thinking? Or do you want to be Jessica Croft, owner of the best dining hall in the state? This poor creature died!"

Jessica was shocked into knowing what she really wanted to do. No, she did not want to be wife to Mr. Grant. He was not her Harry; he was nothing like Harry. Surely there must be another man somewhere more like Harry, someone who Catherine and she could both look up to. But she also wanted to be Jessica Croft. She'd liked her new independence this summer.

It had taken her own dear little girl — no, not such a little girl any more — to show her the true course for the both of them.

She smiled, and reached out to her daughter with a hug. "You're right, my dearest Catherine. 'Out of the mouths of babes' as the Bible says. And I came so close, because I thought I was thinking of you. But of course, I wasn't. I was being weak. Your Da would have said I was forgetting who I am meant to be.

"Anyway, Mr. Grant never laughs, does he? Have you ever heard him laugh?"

Catherine shook her head, her golden hair making a halo as it moved.

"And as the proprietor of the best dining hall in the state," continued Jessica gaily, "perhaps I should create a new dessert just for the two of us, to celebrate. One with a whole pound of raisins, do you think? Remember when I only had a cup of raisins hidden away?"

Catherine began to laugh, and then she sat down abruptly, laughing so hard the tears streamed down her face.

"What on earth is so funny about a pound of raisins?" asked Jessica, smiling with bewilderment.

Catherine controlled her laughter long enough to gasp out, "Mr. Grant is sure to look like a dried-up raisin in a few years, isn't he?"

Jessica was caught up in the merriment. "We'll name our new dessert 'Spotted George' instead of 'Spotted Dick,' like Grandmam's raisin pudding. But for heaven's sakes, lass, don't tell a soul!"

NOTE: recipes from *The Appledore Cookbook,* by M. Parloa. DeWolfe, Fiske and Company, Boston, 1886

The Ten Commandments

Jonathan F. Schmauder

ELEVEN
The Ten Commandments

$\mathcal{E}$laina wanted adventure, a new life, like ones she had read in novels. She had said "no" to every earnest young man who had sought her hand in marriage for over five years, knowing that life with them would be merely a continuation of the boredom that was her life at home with her parents here in Morristown, New Jersey. Her mother didn't understand her reluctance to marry — the young men all had such good prospects, after all — but her father understood completely. He had that yearning for adventure but had stifled it early when he married. He had realized belatedly that one cannot go exploring unknown territory with a wife who even became alarmed when darkness overcame their carriage away from town lights in civilized New Jersey.

So Elaina, now beyond the best age for marriage and with suitors becoming non-existent, answered an ad for a mail-order bride. She studied the ads carefully. What man could be better than a God-fearing preacher? She wrote with the time of her anticipated train arrival in Colorado.

She waited for the train at the Morristown depot with her mother beside her, valiantly trying not to cry; her father grim faced, yet excited at the possibilities his dear daughter would have in the raw land of the West.

Her belongings surrounded her: a trunk full of clothes suitable for rough mining town life in the Colorado Rockies and some for church suppers; a crate containing her grandmother's small rocking chair, crafted by her grandfather; and the most important crate containing the cedar chest her father had made. On the inside of the lid his initials: "J. J. F. 1880, for beloved daughter Elaina Banks French." In the chest were linens, and quilts made by her mother, her aunts, her friends and the church ladies. Colorado nights would be cold.

After days enroute, the train stopped in Carbondale, Colorado. Elaina smoothed her black traveling suit with shaking hands, settled her jaunty hat with the feather more firmly, and stepped forth to meet her promised fiancé.

He was tall and bearded, and more fierce than his photograph had promised. Seeing her, he attempted a smile and bowed slightly. "Miss French? I am the Reverend Haywood Beck. I trust your journey was satisfactory? If you will point out your bag, we will proceed to our nuptials. You are still willing, are you not?"

Elaina decided to ignore the small frisson of doubt that niggled her insides. Might she not rest, wash, don her wedding gown?

As she hesitated, he said, "I'm sorry to be abrupt, Miss French. May I call you Elaine? But we cannot keep the local minister waiting. He must set out on his circuit of small mining camps even as I also ride mine weekly. And it will be a full day's ride to Crystal, causing us to stay overnight on the way."

"Elaina. My name is Elaina. And yes, I am still willing. May I at least wash before the ceremony? I have brought a wedding dress."

"I had thought Elaina a misprint. It is not an American name. Of course you may freshen up in the station. Your traveling outfit is suitable for our wedding. And your bag?"

"I have three boxes."

He frowned. "I do hope you are not a vain woman, Miss French, to bring useless items for your life as an itinerant preacher's wife. My home is small and humble."

Her heart beat hard, and images rose up of what she should do. A mounting clamor within urged her to go more slowly. But her father had always said, "Make up your mind after due thought and stand by your word unless sure knowledge of a mistake presents itself."

She should not go back on her word, though now she was not quite sure.

"I am not vain, but I wish to keep a good home for you."

❦

Thirty minutes after being pronounced man and wife, they jolted over the rough road with her three boxes lashed behind them on the wagon. When darkness approached, they found a rough cabin called an inn and sheltered there for the night.

Reverend Haywood Beck was not a gentle lover, and the next day Elaina sat much of the time with clenched teeth to counter the pain. So this was what marriage was like. But she must cleave unto her husband, as the Bible said.

At the top of a steep, narrow road that descended down the side of a small canyon, the Reverend stopped the horses and went to the back of the wagon. Since he had early on shown he was not inclined to conversation, Elaina merely watched, until she saw him untying her crates. "What are you doing with my boxes, husband?"

"They are far too heavy for the animals for this next part of the road, Mrs. Beck. We will take your clothing and send a man back for the rest."

With panic, Elaina said, "But what will happen to them? Someone may come and make off with them? Please, is there some other way?"

No answer. They drove on.

The brakes squealed on the metal-rimmed wheels. Elaina's only links with home lay behind her in the wilderness. She was miserable. What had she done, to ignore her intuition and marry this man? This was nothing like the books she'd read.

Down and down they went. Soon the sound of a waterfall overlapped the squealing brakes. Above and on the other side of the waterfall was perched a small building with a ladder-like affair descending into the spray below. A maelstrom whirled with logs, debris and foam. She could not rid her mind of the horrifying image.

The road climbed and soon they were among cabins in a narrow valley. Crystal, her new home.

The sun had fallen behind the mountains, and curious miners and a few women chatting with each other looked at her, as the tired horses made their way past the cabins. She smiled and nodded at them, masking her pain and feeling of doom. She would make friends, she knew she would. At the end was a tiny cabin next to a sorry excuse for a church, One would only know what it was by the small unpainted steeple.

"Monday morning I will send for your boxes."

She said nothing, though a small spark of anger nearly made her protest. But sense made her hold her tongue. Arguing would be wasted on this man.

The next day was Sunday, and Elaina dressed well to welcome her husband's flock. The miners greeted her bashfully, the few wives gratefully, and she had the impression this was the largest congregation that had been in this church for some time.

Later in the afternoon a wagon creaked to a stop in front of her little house with her two boxes. The Reverend frowned, and she realized he had sent no one for her boxes. The Sabbath was a day of rest to him, but not to the miners. She was overwhelmingly grateful.

Two of the men opened the boxes and started to lug the chair and the chest into the small cabin. The Reverend stood in the door. "This is the Sabbath. There will be no work in my home. Leave them by the door." The men set the furniture down on the bare dirt, looked away from her, and went to their own cabins.

Elaina couldn't believe he would do this. A cold rain was beginning, and the two pieces would be ruined. She paused for a moment, and then carried her rocking chair inside, placing it to the side of the iron stove opposite the Reverend's chair.

"Wife, I forbade you to do this. I thought you were a God-fearing woman. This is the Sabbath." He stood up from packing his saddlebags and glowered at her.

"And why is your packing not work? I care for these things to honor my father and my mother, and my grandparents. That too is a Commandment. This is not work, this is love."

He struck her then, and she fell to the bed, blood pouring from her nose. "You will not defy me, wife. This is my home and I am your master. You will do as I command."

Elaina sat up, fumbling for a handkerchief to stop the flow of blood. "God is my master, Reverend Beck. And may He have mercy on your soul."

"You dare to tell me my place in your life? Do you think you are a better interpreter of the Word of God than I am; you, a mere woman, and a sinful one at that?" He loomed over her, and she thought he would strike her again. She prepared herself to avoid his hand.

Instead, he turned away, picked up the hatchet by the fireplace, and methodically chopped up her grandmother's lovely little rocking chair. He fed the pieces into the iron stove.

Her soul cracked like frozen glass, and hot anger flowed through her. She would not be graceful in her submission. If he wanted no work done on the Sabbath, neither would she feed him on the Sabbath. She slipped to her knees and began to pray for guidance. Her tears melded with the blood still dribbling from her nose.

When the Reverend Haywood Beck, her husband, said it was time for dinner, she refused. She would not work on the Sabbath because he had commanded it. Cooking was work.

He hit her again, then threw her on the bed. He ripped the buttons off the bodice of her good Sunday dress, and once she was naked he held one hand over her mouth to muffle her cries.

That night Elaina lay unmoving while her husband made animal sounds in his rutting over her body again and again. She bit her lip to keep from crying out with the pain. Thou shalt not kill, she thought. Thou shalt not kill. That is a Commandment too. He will not kill me. I will not let him.

She thought of her parents, how her father had always been so thoughtful of her mother's needs, how he had given up his craving for adventure to love and cherish his family. She finally fell asleep, shivering and bleeding.

She would leave this godless place somehow, and soon. Before she left, the Reverend Haywood Beck would rue the day he made her his whore instead of his true wife. She would wall herself off from him somehow.

In the morning he pulled off her blanket and demanded breakfast before he set out to bring the Word of God to his scattered flock. Not speaking, she complied, though it was hard to walk. When he strode out the door to the shed where the two horses sheltered, she looked out the door to be sure he left the village.

She saw that her cedar chest was gone. So these people did not follow the Commandments either; they had stolen the rest of her life.

It was too much. Elaina crumpled to the floor, sobbing.

After some time, a timid knock sounded, and she roused herself to prevent her neighbors from knowing of her abasement. They brought in Elaina's cedar chest then, dry and filled with her quilts and her memories. They treated her bruises, and the women cried with her, knowing her broken dreams. They knew their stern minister's mind, and they knew his wife needed their help and their friendship. She was not alone after all.

These people knew the way out of this place, though they chose to stay. But then, they did not live with the Reverend Haywood Beck. Elaina sent her cedar chest back to another cabin, to be saved from sure destruction. Meanwhile, her body began to heal. Her soul would take longer.

The Reverend Haywood Beck returned several days later to a silent, unprotesting wife. He thought he had broken her spirit, and she would be a good wife. He had forgotten about her cedar chest and did not miss it.

Would he miss her?

The Coming Storm

TWELVE
The Coming Storm

*A*t last, the grain was ground fine enough to make flat-bread for the evening meal. Morning Light returned from the stone mortar by the lake. As she walked she admired how the peaks of the village tepees echoed the peaks of the Shining Mountains around them. Smoke rose from the campfires, and children laughed and dogs barked as they chased each other.

Morning Light's world was changing, and this worried her. She slapped the dough around more forcefully than necessary. More and more white men were coming to look for gold and silver, and the small band of People had to move from tradi-tional camp sites when they came up to their cool summer land. The whites tore open Mother Earth to dig the shining ores. They made loud explosions, and more than once caused land-slides that altered the land. They wanted land that had been the People's land for generations. Her tribe had to search harder for food, because the animals also had fled the intruders.

Morning Light recited to herself the warnings all the women and girls had been given. *White men lie!* (If one of the People did this, he would be cast out of the tribe.) *White men will take a Ute maiden by force,* (even one as young as she was). *Do not go alone into the lands near the digging men. Keep your knife with you at all times. But when the People meet many white men together, the whites will be kind and they will trade well to get what they want. Learn their language. Our councils will drive them out by peaceful means.*

Despite her dismay at the intruders, Morning Light was drawn to the white people and their way of life, and she had even learned some of their language.

She put the finished dough in a covered pot into the fire to bake.

The next morning, she went down through the trees to see what the white people were doing today. She watched a heavily loaded wagon behind two weary mules struggle up the narrow road that went through the white people's small town. On the bench beside a man sat a woman with hair as pale as her skin. This sad-looking woman wasn't dressed in bright colors like the laughing women who had come in other wagons. A baby wearing a bonnet and a pink calico dress sat in her lap.

From behind the trees the Ute girl followed the wagon to the far edge of the town and up a little track toward the base of the mountain. It was easy for Morning Light to stay hidden. White people had no notion of how to stay invisible among the trees. The man sounded excited to be here as he helped the woman off the wagon and led her to a small log house.

Morning Light was fascinated by the woman with golden hair. She slipped away after her chores during the next days to watch the woman. She saw her chop wood and hang wet clothing on a rope slung between two trees. The baby toddled about, a moving burst of sunshine. Her hair was even whiter than the woman's, and she laughed at everything, even when she fell down. The woman planted seeds, but it was too late to plant. The snows would come within short weeks.

Morning Light wished she could see inside the cabin. At dusk the woman pulled wooden shutters over the windows, and in the daytime calico curtains covered the glass.

One day, still hidden, Morning Light crept closer. She hadn't seen the woman come out of her cabin. The only sounds were the wind in the pine trees and a far off ax chopping wood. She wanted to look inside the cabin. Maybe the woman had gone into town.

"I've seen you skulking around my house," said a woman's hard voice from behind her. "What do you want? To steal something? To take my baby?"

Morning Light whirled, her knife already in her hand. How had this white woman managed to sneak up behind her? Father would be stern when he knew she had let her guard down!

But the white woman looked as frightened as Morning Light, despite the gun she held. The girl dropped her knife as a gesture of friendship. She could reach it quickly enough if the woman tried to take it away. She didn't think the woman would shoot her.

"I do not steal. I do not lie. My name is Morning Light." She tried to make the woman relax, so she smiled. "I like the strength in what I see you do. I know you do not want to be here. I do not want white people here either. But I will be your friend. And I would never take a baby from a mother. I do not lie."

The woman lowered her small handgun and looked at the young Indian girl. "I will believe you because I don't know what else to do. I hate this place. I'm tired of being alone. I don't care about anything but getting Susan away from here, and I have no money to do that." She looked more sad than frightened now.

Morning Light wondered if the woman would mind if she were killed. No, there's the baby. She would fight for it like a mother bear, just as her own mother had died fighting a grizzly to save her.

The woman walked toward her cabin, and Morning Light followed, sheathing her knife on the way. Maybe this sad woman would invite her in and she could see how a white woman lived with her child.

As they walked, the woman said, "Perhaps you can tell me what we're going to eat when snow comes and this pathetic garden I have planted doesn't produce any vegetables. My husband is not making enough money in the mine to keep us from starving."

She turned abruptly to Morning Light, and the girl jumped back, fearful that in her distressed state of mind the woman would hurt her. But instead, she said, "My name is Charlotte Berlin. Come inside. Susan is sleeping."

Morning Light had made up her mind. "I can teach you to find things to eat in the woods, and how to store them when the snow is deep. And I can show you how to set snares for small animals. I can keep you from starving. But my people will leave here soon for our winter hunting grounds. If you want me to teach you it must be soon."

And so it was agreed. In the next few weeks, Morning Light taught Charlotte Berlin ways to survive in the high country woods. In return, the white woman invited her into her cabin. She let her hold the sweet-smelling child, who explored the fringe on Morning Light's dress and then wriggled to be set down to play on the dirt floor with a rag doll.

Charlotte showed Morning Light the wonders she had brought with her from what she called civilization. Delicate china tea cups, with little plates to go under them, and a drink of China tea — the last of her supply, she said. A looking glass that showed Morning Light her real face, not the one that wavered in lake water. There were fine linens for bedding, with a big bag full of goose feathers to sleep under in the cold nights. A book held photographs of the family she had left behind, somewhere called Back East.

The two became close friends, though Dieter Berlin was not happy about it. But he soon got over his hesitation, and one day asked to go to the camp with Morning Light, to meet her father and trade for some dried venison. Charlotte looked at him with a frown, but said nothing. Morning Light remembered the warnings about white men alone with a Ute woman, but she ignored her unease and led him toward the camp. After all, he was her friend's husband, not a stranger.

On the way, they saw a black bear foraging in a berry patch. Dieter Berlin pulled Morning Light to him. "If we stand together we will look large enough to be a threat, and she will go away," he whispered.

Morning Light knew that the bear, which was probably a male because of his size, would go away by himself if they didn't move. She saw no cubs nearby to protect. She said a silent prayer to the bear to make him realize she and Dieter Berlin were not his enemies.

The bear looked up as the faint wind shifted and he smelled the humans. He reared up on his hind legs, but decided there was no threat. Because he was well fed this late in the summer, he ambled off in the other direction.

Dieter Berlin let his breath out slowly. He still kept a strong grip on Morning Light's arm. With the other hand she prepared to reach for her knife, just in case. He looked down on her. "You're just a little thing, aren't you? But not too little to be friendly."

He bent down to kiss her, but Morning light was quicker. Her knife was in her hand and under his chin. "I do not want to hurt you because Charlotte is my friend, but I will use this knife if you do not let me go."

He didn't move. Then he pushed her away forcibly, and she nearly fell. "Well, I guess you savages have gumption if nothing else." He laughed. "Okay, you got me beat. I didn't mean any harm. Just being friendly. No hard feelings, okay?"

She was meant to think he was innocent of bad thoughts. But his eyes glittered with malice. Morning Light was thankful her camp was close.

She didn't want to lose her friendship with Charlotte and Susan.

"I will say nothing to Charlotte or my father this time, but next time your scalp will decorate my tepee."

He laughed again at this threat, but he looked uneasy. He glanced around to see if any other natives were creeping up on them. "Are we close to your camp? I should get this dickering over with and get back to supper."

She turned and led the way, being sure to stay a good distance in front of him. Her hand stayed on the handle of her knife.

About a week later, as Morning Light came near the Berlins' cabin with a handful of watercress from a nearby stream, she saw a horse and buggy drive up the dirt road. Two stern ladies dressed in black went inside. Alarmed because of their expressions, Morning Light went quietly to the nearest window.

"People are talking, Mrs. Berlin," she heard one of the women saying. "You have that filthy savage girl around your house at all hours of the day. It isn't healthy and it isn't civilized. She will bring the braves back with her in the dark of the night, mark my words, and they will murder you and your husband in your bed. They will lift your scalps and adorn their heathen tepees with your blonde hair. They think yellow hair hanging on their war shields will keep them safe in their battles.

"And," added the other harsh-voiced woman, "they will take little Susan. She will grow up a slave and have to marry some heathen Indian."

Morning Light felt her hackles rise. How could those ignorant women say this! They lied! None of her people would do such things. She had even made a doll for little Susan out of a piece of buckskin. Her father said it was good and honorable for her to teach the white woman to survive the winter. It would make the townspeople realize the People were friends.

Without waiting to hear more, Morning Light put the watercress on the chopping block near the woodpile, where it would be found, and crept back into the woods.

♛

That night a sudden blizzard struck. The People had stayed too long, although they had been packing for their trek out of the high mountains. Now they must wait until the storm blew itself out. With luck they would find a path before winter closed them in for good. If that happened, they would go hungry, despite their supplies of dried venison and pemmican, just as some of the whites surely would starve.

The wind howled through the trees and the snow fell until there were at least four feet on the ground, with great drifts everywhere. Leaves were still on the aspens, and the snow bowed them down. The People had snowshoes made of birch with leather thongs so they could walk, although the snow was too deep for horses.

The medicine man said a warm spell was coming. They would be able to walk out of the mountains when most of the snow melted.

Morning Light worried about Charlotte and her baby. She had seen no snowshoes in the cabin. Dieter Berlin wouldn't have been able to get to the mine in the snowstorm, however, so Charlotte and Susan would not be alone. Morning Light had told Charlotte that she would be leaving before heavy snow, and the woman would not expect her to come again. Morning Light felt a pang of sorrow. She would not be wanted any more either, not after what those women had said.

The weather warmed so rapidly in the next few days that the men of the Ute camp worried about the heavy snow.

Morning Light was in her tepee sharpening her knife when she heard a great roar filling the whole valley. Booming noises meant huge trees were falling.

Avalanche!

The Ute village was well placed, and the snow above them did not move. But the last cabins in the town were not in a good place.

Charlotte! Baby Susan! Morning Light leapt up. She must rescue her friends. She grabbed a heavy fur coat and deerskin mittens as she raced out of the tepee. She shouted to the men at a campfire. "Quickly! We must help my friend and her baby. Their home is in the path of the snow, I am sure."

She bent to put on snowshoes that had been leaning against the tepee.

Her father came and took her arms gently. "Child, there has been too much heavy snow falling. Half the town will be covered, too deep to find your friends. There is no use. Calm yourself." He looked at his favorite child, his oldest, and he saw her panic.

"Father, you would try to dig out our village if this had happened, no matter how deep the snow. Charlotte is my friend." She was shaking now.

"That is different. The white people do not want us here. They will dig each other out of the snow."

"The Berlin cabin is away from the others. They won't get to her and the baby until it is too late. If I don't go, she will know those women were right about our people."

Her father nodded then, and called to the others Morning Light ran clumsily toward the town on her snowshoes. Soon warriors passed her. Her father caught her hand to help her run faster. As she ran, she sang a silent prayer to the snow so that it would give up its victims, her friends.

The cabin was buried except for a front corner. Much of the town was devastated. Here and there people were digging where there must be houses, though now much was white tumbled snow and shattered trees.

Morning Light shouted to Charlotte Berlin, hoping she could hear. If she were alive.

The village men had brought implements for digging. Morning Light dug with her hands where she knew the door was until her lungs burned and her hands were nearly frozen inside her sopping mittens. At last she touched wood. Her father shouldered her aside, and pounded on the door. It wouldn't open, and there was no sound from inside.

Someone struck the door with an ax. Finally it splintered enough for them to get through.

Morning Light went inside and heard little Susan's frightened cry. The place was filled with a jumble of snow and overturned furniture. She could see no life, but she headed for the sound of the child. "I am here, little Susan; it is Morning Light. We will find you. Tell me where you are."

The child called out, "Mama! Mama!"

The men dug frantically. They uncovered the child under a turned-over chair. Morning Light took the cold little girl and hugged her. She had left her own coat outside, but one of the women came in with it to wrap the baby.

Morning Light turned back to look for Charlotte. A fresh tumble of snow cascaded toward her as one of the men moved the overturned table. She saw an arm. They all dug with their hands, breaths ragged from their efforts.

They uncovered Charlotte at last. She was unconscious but breathing. The women helped Morning Light drag her outside, and they wrapped her with their warm coats, rubbed her skin to bring her back to life. Little Susan hugged her mother, calling, "Mama! Play with Susan!"

Charlotte finally stirred. She looked at her child, then at Morning Light and the circle of women around her, now all smiling and congratulating each other on having found her. She put her hand out to Morning Light and whispered, "Thank you, friend."

Inside the cabin, the men still searched for Dieter Berlin, and Morning Light went to help.

They found him under the upturned cabinet. He was bleeding from sharp wood splinters and shards of broken dishes, but he was still alive.

But the heavy cabinet had pinned his legs under it. There was blood everywhere.

With a great deal of effort and frantic digging, the men managed to move the cabinet enough so that the man could be pulled out from under it. His legs were crushed, and bones protruded from his bloody trousers. He had not been wearing shoes. His feet no longer looked like feet. The pain of the move and the new loss of blood made him cry out, though he was still unconscioius.

What were they to do? The medicine man, who had been looking at Charlotte and little Susan, came inside to where Dieter Berlin lay. He looked at the blood on the cold floor and shook his head.

Morning Light said, "You must save him. He is my friend's husband."

"He will not live because he will not want to live as a cripple," the medicine man said. "But I will stop the blood loss." With rawhide thongs he bound each leg above the shattered portion, and the blood flow lessened to a mere trickle. He cut off the remains of the man's pants and sprinkled dried herbs on the mutilated flesh, whispering incantations as he worked. He wrapped the broken flesh with moss and cloth. "This is all I can do. The rest is up to the Great Spirit."

♕

Morning Light's father and his men moved down the buried road to join the search for more victims, and the medicine man went with them. Morning Light and several women stayed with the Berlins. They hoped that Charlotte, lying outside where she couldn't see her husband, would be strong enough to bear the news. They could see that she would have another baby, most likely in the early spring. They kindled a fire from shattered cabin logs, and someone had thought to bring food. Something hot would help the injured couple.

What could a woman do in this place with a crippled husband, Morning Light wondered? They had no more home, and they could not fix the roof until the snow melted.

The other townspeople would take them in, she decided. Charlotte would not have to fend for herself. Surely white people cared for women whose husbands could not work, just as the People did.

Morning Light went back inside to Dieter Berlin, where one of the women watched. His breathing was fitful, though it soon grew stronger. Suddenly he opened his eyes and stared at her.

"I can't move my legs," he said. "I can't even feel them. What happened?"

"The avalanche buried you under the big dish cabinet. Both of your legs are crushed. Our medicine man has stopped the bleeding. You will live." Morning Light didn't see any sense in keeping this information from him. She still thought of the look in his eyes when he had tried to attack her, but then she felt ashamed of her anger. He was her friend's husband.

"People in the town will help you and your family. They will care for you. Charlotte is strong. She will work in the town to keep her family together."

Outside, Morning Light could hear little Susan laughing as one of the village girls played with her. Charlotte's voice rose, demanding to know what had happened to her husband.

Dieter Berlin heard her too. Suddenly he grabbed Morning Light's arm and pulled her to him with surprising strength. Knife in hand, Morning Light hesitated. The other woman had her knife out too, but waited for a signal from Morning Light. She couldn't understand what the man was saying.

"That's right, you pretty little thing. I know how strong you are. Use that knife on me. You must. Or let me bleed again. Charlotte doesn't want no cripple for a husband. She could never make do if she had me to take care of. I'm as good as dead. Don't let me die this way, inch by inch. You're her friend. Help her this way."

Morning Light pulled back against his grasp, horrified. Kill him? How could she do such a thing? She could kill only to save her own life. How could she kill a crippled man?

He saw the hesitation in her eyes, and he jerked her closer to him, though he grimaced with the pain his sharp movement caused.

"If you don't do this, I'll tell everyone I had my way with you in the woods that day, and you loved it. I'll tell Charlotte. She'll believe me. Everyone will believe me." His breathing was harsh and rapid, but his grip was strong.

Morning Light's eyes widened with the shock of what he said. Her heart began to race. She thought of her friend and little Susan.

"What you do with your body is for you to decide," she finally said, looking at him with a new hardness on her face. "You can reach the leather thongs around your legs. I will not help you."

She turned her back on him, and took the other woman outside.

The sun was shining now, and the heavy snow dripped as it melted on the trees that were still standing. The village woman talked about where to take Charlotte and Dieter Berlin. Morning Light knelt by Charlotte, who was feeding little Susan hot soup.

If Dieter told Charlotte lies about the day in the woods, he would shatter her faith in him, already weakened by her forced move from her family. But Charlotte would do whatever it would take to be sure little Susan thrived. There was nothing Morning Light could do about Dieter Berlin.

But she could still be a friend to Charlotte. What if Dieter Berlin died before the tribe left the mountains? Could she stay with her friend, to help and support her?

Yes, she would do that, though her father and the tribe might not approve. Perhaps she could convince her people it would help them if she learned more of the whites' ways.

Charlotte was strong enough to stand up now, and she walked toward the remains of her cabin, leaving Susan with Morning Light. The snow was blinding white in the sun.

From the ruined cabin came a cry that split the snow-muffled valley.

Safe

THIRTEEN
Safe

*T*he minute Bran walked into the Gold Dust Saloon, I could see he was one of those rare men who glow with an inner light. His charisma left people mesmerized. He noticed me that first night, but though his glance quickened, he didn't speak to me until several days had passed, as if studying the feasibility of approaching me. Of course, I had my hands full, as usual, being the piano player, and having to fend off heavy-handed louts every so often who wanted to carry me up the stairs as if I were one of those girls.

Bran came to my rescue finally, when one man more persistent than usual kept his chair pulled too close to my piano stool. I had been watching Bran too, and was glad to have a protector. He was so entrancing that I was smitten right away. All of the other women in the place went addle-pated when he looked at them. When he looked at a woman she was the center of his universe. It's hard to break away from that kind of attention.

He told me he had come from the East with the deed to a silver mine his brother had left him. The mines are hard teachers; the brother had died in a cave-in. When a rock slide crippled Bran, he came to work behind the table in the saloon. No one seemed to be bothered by that limp. It added to his aura of mystery.

I knew the tunes I played so well I didn't have to watch my hands on the keys, so I could watch Bran at the gambling tables. He dealt the cards as if born to the craft, shining his luminescent smile on the men who knew there had to be one lucky card just waiting to make them winners. They gave up their hard-won pokes of gold to him, and he laughed and told them they would win the next time, never mind if they lost tonight. They believed him. They believed anything he told them.

I believed him too. When Bran proposed, I gladly left my life of playing for the clutching men in the saloon. We married, and I bore him a perfect small child, a tiny daughter exquisite in every way, but born too soon. We buried Celeste in the meadow above the town, among the buttercups. The scent of the mountain pines drifted into the small casket before the soil hid my child from the sunlight. Bran's smile dimmed for awhile, but not for long.

It took me longer to recuperate and to let the pain diminish. I wanted to cling to him, but my shining knight spent more and more hours away from home. I waited for him in our small wooden house and rocked my grief away.

Bran tried to rekindle my passion, but my body was numb too. In his hurt, he accused me of disgust for his crippled leg. I couldn't make him understand my anguish over the loss of little Celeste. After a time, he slept on the sofa. He came home later and later. I mourned that too, even though there was scarce room in my broken heart for this second loss.

One night I was awakened by a slammed door and a laugh I didn't recognize. I put on my wrapper and went into the parlor. Bran had brought a young girl, surely no more than nine or ten. Her face was wan and pinched, though she had been laughing with him. Now she looked worried. He turned from her with her coat in his hand, and limped toward me with his radiant smile.

"Now you don't need to mourn the baby any more, my love. I've brought you another child to mother. I rescued her from Sparky's crib in the Nugget Saloon. Too young to be in the hands of those rough miners, don't you think, my dear? Her name is Mercy."

This precious child in a whore's bed? At last my frozen heart began to thaw, and I looked at her intently. She blushed, and looked down at the floor, where a puddle spread itself from the snow caked on her thin leather boots. I hugged her and welcomed her to our family.

Bran and I carried the trundle that would have been our daughter's into the small storage room, and I made up the bed for the child. I watched as Mercy climbed under the covers, clad in an old shift of mine. She smiled sleepily and soon slept.

In the next days Mercy helped me rearrange and clean the room, and she took delight in claiming it as hers. She hadn't wanted to be a whore, she said, but her father had sold her to Sparky. She heard later he was killed in a mine explosion. Her mother had died when she was born. The poor lamb had no one, but now she had us.

Mercy and I shopped at the mercantile for calico and sprigged muslin and fine wool, which we sewed into decent dresses for her. She could barely read, so I gave her lessons in reading and ciphering. The child blossomed until she looked healthy and calm, not nervous and pinched as she had on that cold night.

One night I wakened to strange muffled sounds, not like those husband made when he returned from his gaming table. I went by dim moonlight to Mercy's door and opened it. My heart froze. Bran was on top of the child, and her hands were tied to the bedstead. His hand was over her mouth. Silently I crept up behind him, gripped his neck and wrenched him from his pleasure. I tried hard to strangle him, but he was too strong.

After I had cut Mercy loose and stopped her sobbing, I chased Bran from the house all the way to the saloon with a butcher knife from the kitchen drawer. For a wonder, the moon had set and no one saw me, or I surely would have been locked up as a crazy woman.

When I got home, I bathed my daughter in heated water and dressed her in her new blue wool dress and a warm cloak. I went to Bran's hiding place for his poker winnings, under the third brick on the right side of the fireplace grate. I reckoned the money was mine, after what he had done. I took it all. We set out before dawn with the horse and a few belongings tied in a bundle.

When we reached Denver some time later, I opened a school with that money. I had a piano brought to the schoolhouse, and I taught the children to sing. I discovered Mercy had a lovely clear high voice.

As Mercy grew up, I was afraid to let her go off on her own, thinking her ethereal beauty and glorious voice were a recipe for disaster. I booked the two of us into fine entertainment centers in Denver. I played for Mercy, and she charmed listeners with her voice. She even caught the attention of critics from the East.

But she would not leave Denver. She loved the backdrop of the Rocky Mountains, visible from our suite in the Brown Palace. I loved their distance, and the distance from the mining camps, because I couldn't forget the treachery of Bran. Yet he had brought me Mercy, and for that I was thankful.

One night a large bouquet of red roses was delivered to Mercy's dressing room. This was nothing new. Mercy had many admirers, but none so far had touched her heart. She was very wary of men, and avoided them when she could. Her short time in Sparky's had made her unable to trust any man. Bran had not helped.

The card with the roses read, "To the most beautiful and talented young woman in the West." Again, nothing new. No one appeared at her door after the performance.

The next night, another bouquet with the same card, but this time the roses were white. No one came again. Mercy's anxiety grew, and she jumped at sharp noises.

The third night, a card was delivered, but no flowers. It read, "I will deliver your bouquet after I hear your glorious voice once again, and then we will go to a light supper. You may bring your mama."

Mercy was intrigued now, I could tell, but I didn't have a good feeling about this enigmatic suitor. Mercy needed a man who would care for her, one who would cherish and protect her as I had done. This man sounded manipulative, a man of the world.

She sang like an angel that night. I could tell she was searching the crowded auditorium for her admirer as she sang. Still, her performance was flawless, perhaps the best she had ever given. She received a standing ovation.

Back in the dressing room, Mercy's color was high. "Maybe we should go to supper with this man, Mama. He might be nice, and he isn't pushy! But you must come too. I would never go with a stranger alone."

"We shall see. It depends on what I think of him, my dearest." I helped her change her gown. But I worried.

A knock at the door. I waited until she had patted her hair into place, watched her eyes sparkling with anticipation.

When I opened the door, there was Bran. I heard Mercy suck in her breath.

I should have expected him to show up after he heard of Mercy's great success. My heart plummeted, and I was frozen, with the doorknob still in my hand.

That inner glow was as brilliant as ever.

I made to shut the door in his face, wrenched free of my shock at last.

"No, Mama. Let him come in. We have things to discuss."

What could she mean? Horrified, I turned to look at my child, and saw a child no longer. Her face was white, and it was hard. Her mouth, usually curved in a sweet smile, was straight and firm.

Bran came in with words of apology for neglecting us for so long, with praise for Mercy's voice, her looks. Did he have no shame? But still he glowed with promises he could never keep, not after what he had done to us both.

He bent to kiss my Mercy.

She dealt him such a blow that blood came from his nose. Then she hitched up her dress and kicked the man hard between the legs. He collapsed on the dressing room floor, retching.

I was astounded! My gentle Mercy had done this?

Mercy went past me to the door and called the security man. "This man," she said to the astonished guard, "has made an obscene advance. Have him arrested. He is never to come near me again."

We gathered our wraps and swept out of the room, leaving two men to carry out the miserable Bran, once light of my life.

Mercy smiled at me as we walked. "I did learn some useful things in Sparky's crib, Mama. But as you can see, I am no longer a child."

I smiled back at her, and a bittersweet feeling filled my breast. My child had begun to see the complexities of adult life, but I wondered if this would be the end of Bran.

Forbidden Stitch

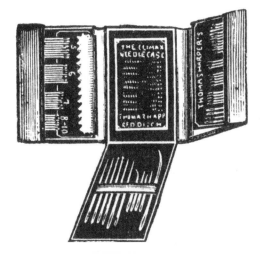

FOURTEEN
Forbidden Stitch

*A*h Song looked at the filthy miner, but she did not meet his eyes. That would not be proper. She looked at the worn, dirt-colored pants and shirt on the counter and wrote down on a piece of paper the harsh-sounding American name he told her loudly. He must have thought she was deaf instead of merely mute by choice.

The miner pulled out one of the pockets and shouted, "Hole in the pocket. Can you fix it?"

Ah Song nodded yes and dismissed the man by turning her back on him. She carried the bundle into the sewing room, holding it well away from her clean blue jacket and trousers. Pigs, these white miners were!

She suppressed a sigh, taking strength in her silence and dismissing the miner and all others like him from her mind. Trying not to think of Pao-Lin was a more difficult task. If only her husband had not been killed by that thieving giant of a railroad crew overseer. He had been given no chance to defend himself — a blow to the back of his head had killed him instantly. The brute had stolen what little cash Pao-Lin had been carrying, money the couple had been saving to send home to their aging parents in China. Money they had earned working on the vast railroad that was spanning this continent.

Ah Song shuddered and stared at the bare rocky peak above the mining camp as she thought of the night the killer had come to her tent as she slept, looking for more money. Disguised as a boy so she could enter the country, she had used *tai chi* to save herself from being raped after the man had ripped off her clothing. She left the man unconscious, though she'd hated him enough to kill him.

Early the next morning Ah Song had found a quiet spot behind a hill away from the work site. She needed to clear her mind of hatred. As she practiced the gentle, flowing movements of *tai chi,* she heard a sound. She whirled, ready to defend herself again. The man had followed her. This time he died.

Ah Song fled to the mountains. Killing with *tai chi* was forbidden, unless necessary to save one's life and honor. But ending someone's life did bother her, though necessary to save her honor and perhaps her life. And she knew the authorities would not believe her word that the killing had been in self-defense. She was only a Chinese worker, next to worthless.

Now, far away in the mountains south of the railroad construction and openly female, Ah Song felt almost safe, except for one question: could she be traced here, to this primitive place? Could she be arrested for murder?

Ah Song wanted to stay here in this mountain camp, at least for now. The forest and the streams here were harmonious. But sometimes the tall mountains with their unyielding rocky heights made her uneasy. Above the treeline, they were harsh and unforgiving. She tried not to look up at those bare peaks.

Nor did she want to spend all of her life mending and washing men's filthy clothes. She would only stay until she had money to return to China.

Ah Song forced these thoughts out of her mind and sat down in her sewing cubicle, close to the steamy wash room. She put a clean cloth on her lap and pulled the torn pants pocket out so she could mend it carefully. Her eyes were better than they had been when she had been forced to use the Forbidden Stitch on delicate silk robes for the royal family in China. Each fine stitch, a perfect knot the size of a poppy seed, had strained Ah Song's eyes and given her fierce headaches.

Now all her stitches were once again proper and infinitesimally small, and miners as well as dance hall girls sought her services. Ah Song stitched up the hole in the pocket. Then she pulled out the other pocket, to see if it too needed restitching.

A glint of something yellow fell onto the white cloth in her lap. What could this be? She turned closer to the window.

Gold dust? She looked more closely. She put a small grain in a glass of water. It sank rapidly.

Was this the answer to her prayers, the means of her escape? She carefully collected the shiny grains in the center of the cloth. She found more dust in the pocket of the dirty shirt. Her small lacquered box, the only treasure she still had left from China, would hold these precious morsels.

When the miner came back — if he did not die in one of the common mine cave-ins or explosions — he would bring her two pockets' worth of dust, grains that he would overlook but she would not. Other miners' clothing must hold similar treasures.

Ah Song finished mending the pants and several rips in the shirt. She carried them to the washroom, where the girl with few wits washed the clothing methodically. She smiled at the girl, whose name was Mary. Ah Song idly wondered if she should take Mary with her when she made her way out of these mountains. But then what would she do with her? She could not take the girl to China; she was an ugly foreigner.

But could she leave her here, at the mercy of Red Harris, the master of the laundry and the mercantile next door? He frequented the girls upstairs in the saloon, but when Ah Song had arrived, he had looked her up and down most insolently. She didn't trust him. Mary probably didn't have the wits to fend him off.

Mary was a cheerful young woman, and she always seemed anxious to be friends with Ah Song. The two of them sometimes ate together. Mary could never master the art of eating with chopsticks, but had to eat her noodles from the Chinese café with a fork. She tried hard not to be a messy eater, and Ah Song appreciated her efforts.

Ah Song watched the sweaty girl pull scrubbed miners' clothing out of the suds with her reddened hands. Another thought occurred to her

What treasures might lurk in the bottom of the wash tub? She would help Mary with the wash, or at least with the emptying of the tub. She would keep the secret from the girl somehow — Mary wouldn't be able to keep her mouth silent.

Ah Song decided she had to break her vow of silence. "Go to the mercantile, Mary, and bring more soap. I will empty the tub for you. Go."

Mary looked at her, shocked because Ah Song had spoken to her after weeks of silence. But then she became quite agitated, and she began to cry.

Perhaps Mary had already found gold in the wash water! Ah Song comforted her with smiles and quiet words. In broken whispers, Mary told Ah Song her secret: yes, there was gold dust in miners' clothing. She was saving what she found to buy a kitten.

She had known how to hold her tongue after all. Ah Song had been good to her, and now she would share her secret. Ah Song told Mary she too liked kittens.

She talked to Mary when no one was around, and they whispered about their growing horde of gold while the summer came and deepened.

One night in early September, the two women stole silently away from the camp, hiding under the tarpaulin in the wagon of a supplier who had come up from the city. Once there, Ah Song rented a small room for the two of them. Mary needed better clothing for what Ah Song planned. She must look like a woman who could afford a servant. She must learn how to walk as if she were important. Ah Song would be right behind her, would protect her.

Ah Song steeled herself as they walked into the railroad station. Surely two women, even if one were Chinese and somewhat despised because of that, would be safe. And she had *tai chi*. Still, better to become invisible than to make a scene anywhere in this land of tall, loud men. Mary was happy to follow Ah Song's directions, walking slightly in front of her as if the Chinese woman were her servant. She pretended she was in a play.

When they arrived some time later in San Francisco, they took some time to look around the busy city. What she saw made Ah Song decide she would not go to China. She could send money from here to her family. Gold was right here in different forms, and there would be many ways to accumulate it.

What could be a better place for two enterprising women, even if one were a Chinese woman who had killed, and the other one less simple than she seemed? Ah Song would make beautiful clothing with fine embroidery. Americans would pay much gold for the Forbidden Stitch, work traditionally done only for royalty. Mary would help tend Ah Song's shop, in which they would sell treasures from China, ready to be bought by rich Americans.

First of all, she and Mary found two kittens to keep in their rooms over the shop.

The wharves were in San Francisco Bay and near Ah Song's shop, some distance from the ocean. After several months, when her shop was becoming profitable, Ah Song traveled to a beach on the ocean one morning to practice *tai chi*. As she began the movements, staring into the fog-muted waves, she thought back to the mining camp in the mountains.

She remembered the flowing wind moving the tall trees, and the clear stream water that flowed above the mining site, where it became sad, muddied and polluted. She might have stayed in the mountains and taken the graceful strength of the trees for her own; she could have learned from the water as it glided around and over the rocks.

But the rocky masses of the mountains she had fled were too solid; her *chi* had felt trapped between their sharp peaks and unyielding masses.

Here on this San Francisco beach Ah Song was a part of the ocean with its incessant surf dashing against the new land she had chosen, just as it threw itself against the shore of her birthplace. She wondered if any bit of water that lapped at her feet would flow with the mighty ocean currents and sigh upon the shores of China.

The fresh damp tang of the air and the spray of the waves helped center Ah Song. Here the energy of the rugged land entered her, and the *chi* of the place re-aligned itself with periodic shakings of the earth.

Ah Song's movements flew faster and faster; sweat beaded her body, and she finished with a triumphant intensity just as the sun behind her pierced the fog and turned everything golden.

Megan's Mountains

FIFTEEN
Megan's Mountains

*T*he first thing Megan O'Sullivan did when she arrived in Colorado was buy a mule, a sensible sort who never put his ears back. She named him Newton, after a favorite, mild-mannered uncle. Megan wanted to learn what she could about the craft of coaxing precious gold from the earth. She headed uphill on a narrow path to a mine she'd heard about above the town, carrying a shovel, a pickax, a small tent and some food. The day was warm and Megan began to sweat. She had stopped to drink from her canteen when, from the other side of a gigantic boulder, she heard a quarrelsome voice spouting scripture.

"'And the earth was without form, and void and darkness was upon the face of the deep. And the spirit of God moved upon the face of the waters.'" The querulous voice continued, "But it ought to be The Old Man moved out of the waters and up to the mountains. You get wet in the water; the mountains are the first step to Heaven." A creaking laugh, and then some mumbling.

Megan wondered if she was about to meet a madman. She put her hand on her holster.

The man came around the boulder and stopped dead when he saw her and Newton, who whickered softly at the man's small burro. "What in tarnation are you doing up here, woman? And in men's pants! 'Who can find a virtuous woman? Strength and honor are her clothing.'"

Megan stiffened. Men had looked askance at her clothing in the town, and she had to expect this sort of thing. "I dress for what I do. I'm aiming to mine for gold, and I can't do that in a dress, now can I?"

The man's skin was copper-colored from the sun, his beard was unkempt and mostly a dirty white, and his clothes looked as if they hadn't seen a washing for a year.

They stood there sizing up each other. Then he pulled off his hat and whacked it on his leg, causing a great cloud of dust to rise. He laughed and said, "I might be persuaded to teach you how to use all that fancy equipment you got weighing down that poor mule. Though you might need more than a tent, a shovel and a pick. You must think the gold is going to jump out of the mountain. "For a half share I'll be your partner," he continued, trying to look lofty but failing. "And you do the cooking. We'll look at a likely place I just passed, and then go down for proper gear."

He turned his burro around without waiting for a reply and started off uphill again.

Megan went after him. "Hold on there, old timer! I don't plan to share with anyone for the long run, but I'll share until you teach me how to mine. Then I'm off on my own. And I choose the places to dig."

He stopped and looked back, frowning. "What makes you think you know better than me where to dig? You been out in these hills for forty years like I have? I was here before you were born, Missy!"

He mustn't learn about my voices, Megan thought warily. So she only said, "I have my ways. I don't want to waste my time digging where there's no gold. Obviously you haven't done so well all those forty years, or you'd be sitting in a fancy hotel suite in Denver eating oysters and caviar."

He frowned at her for another minute and said, "'The discourse of fools is irksome.' I'll give you one chance to prove your method."

He showed Megan how to uncover and fracture the white quartz outcropping with her pickax, but it gave them nothing in the way of gold even after several hours of breaking it up to look for a seam. Megan kept waiting for her intuition, as she called those murmuring voices, to tell her she was on the track of gold, but the voices remained silent.

The two of them headed back to town.

"I don't want to work in streams with pans and sluices and rockers, being wet all the time," Megan told the old man as they walked. "I love the idea of being up high, burrowing into the mountains, finding ore in nooks and crannies, even if it means I have to blast it out."

Megan bought picks, drills, shovels, sledgehammers, crowbars, dynamite and yards of fuse — everything Homer Beaufort, prospector, mountain man, Bible-spouting ex-minister told her she should have for mining.

Back in the mountains, Megan's strange intuition directed her to her first tunnel. They struck a good lode in their first shaft. They slaved every moment of daylight.

Megan knew she would have trouble getting rid of Homer Beaufort, who became more and more enthusiastic as the tunnel kept producing ore-bearing quartz. He was entertaining, persistent and he knew the craft.

Homer was surprised at Megan O'Sullivan's strength with a pickax and shovel, her tenacity, her ability to find good veins. The altitude never slowed her down, even though it left him complaining. "'Though I have all faith, so that I could remove mountains' obviously I don't have enough faith and never did, or I wouldn't be here hanging on to the coattails of a female. For God's sake, woman, slow down! I can't dig an inch if I get up this here mountain on my knees!"

So Megan learned to slow down walking uphill. She grew strong, but it was hard to be doing much of the work alone. She even chopped down the trees needed to shore up the tunnels. Homer's energy was not as great as he bragged, though he was wiry and hard. Once he went on his own way, Megan knew she would have to devise ways to hold the iron drill in place so that she could strike it with the heavy sledge hammer. She learned to pour blasting powder carefully in the drilled hole, with a long length of fuse in the middle of it.

The first time Megan set a blast in the mine, Homer waited outside the tunnel. He had been hard pressed to suppress his mirth as he showed her where to set the drill and how to put in the dynamite and a long long fuse. Megan couldn't figure out the joke, but she knew she would find out the hard way.

She lit the fuse and ran as fast as she could toward the entrance, but not quickly enough. The concussion knocked her down. Rocks came flying after her, and she was covered with fine dust. Homer cackled at her as she lay sprawled in the tunnel, but he helped her get up anyway. Megan learned to run faster.

♛

Most of the miners left Megan O'Sullivan alone. They all knew Homer, and they figured he was no threat to their mining claims, but they shied away from Megan. She was a woman and there was something odd in a woman who dressed in miners' clothing and wanted to dig a mine on her own.

They decided the first good mine she drilled was a lucky fluke. Still, they grumbled, it wasn't right; she was only a woman, not a real miner like they were.

But they also realized Megan O'Sullivan was a tough customer. She wouldn't take any strong-arming from a man. She would get a hard look in her eyes, and her jaw muscles would twitch, and then she would tell them in no uncertain terms where they could take their ideas. Her hand would stray suspiciously close to the .45 she carried. She was obviously the boss, and Homer merely the hired hand. They watched the old geezer argue half-heartedly with her, apparently just for form, and then he'd go right off and do what she said.

There was a big to-do at the assay office when she went to record her first claim. Women weren't supposed to do that. It had never been done. But when Megan drew her revolver and laid it on the counter, the startled clerk changed his mind. The story got out, and men tipped their hats when they saw her.

She called her first mine the Megan. The claim paper she kept hidden so no one would steal it while she was in her tunnel.

That first strike opened up a vein several feet wide, and word got out. Soon she began hearing explosions where other miners had staked claims near hers. But they didn't always succeed — they didn't have Megan's voices to guide them.

A few misguided souls came calling, thinking to talk her into sharing her claim. The first time this happened, Megan had just cooked up a mess of beans over her campfire, and she and Homer were sitting down on a log to eat. She was in no mood to be sociable. The law of the mountains said she must share her campfire, so she begrudgingly offered the two men some beans. They ate heartily, glad for food someone else had cooked. Megan didn't try to keep the conversation going when it veered to her mine. Instead, she washed out her tin dish and utensils before propping up a few empty sarsaparilla bottles on a stump. She walked off a goodly way and pulled out her handgun. The bottles shattered one after the other. The men looked at each other. Homer sat on his log grinning and smoking his smelly pipe that kept going out, making quite a show of having to relight it.

Megan walked back to the stump and set up a couple of beer bottles. This time she picked up her rifle and walked several hundred feet away in a different direction. All three men moved hastily away from where they had been sitting. The beer bottles exploded one after the other.

The miners decided they needed to get back to their holdings before dark, and they high-tailed it out of the camp. Megan smiled at Homer, who chortled and danced around like a crazy man as the disgruntled prospectors walked off into the dusk. Word got around, and the question of sharing her mine never came up again.

When the aspen leaves began to turn to a golden yellow, Megan decided she didn't like the idea of sharing a cabin with Homer. He stank to high heaven even when he wasn't sweating. She had never seen him bathe or wash his clothes in all the months she'd known him.

She talked him into wintering in town. He could come back up in the spring, she said, when it was warm enough for him to stay in his tent. He didn't argue, except to give dire predictions about avalanches. His parting words, delivered as he hobbled off down the trail leading Dolly, were, "'Therefore will we not fear, though the earth be removed, and though the mountains be carried into the midst of the sea.'"

Megan decided that was supposed to reassure her.

Feeling free again for the first time in months, she built a tight little cabin close to the Megan Mine. She and Newton hauled supplies up from the town. She became a familiar sight, walking down the hill with Newton laden with gold-bearing ore, then going back up with the two of them loaded with food for the winter. Laying in big sacks of flour, onions, potatoes, and smaller bags of other necessaries kept her busy for a few weeks.

Every time Megan came down to town in those early fall days, she found Homer watching for her. She had grown fond of the irascible old goat, even as she chafed at having him around. He had little money of his own, Megan had discovered, so she always bought him a good meal. In thanks for his invaluable lessons in mining, she opened a special account for him at the bank.

Homer was suspicious and refused to take the bankbook at first.

"It's a retainer, Homer," Megan explained patiently. "People do this in the business world. It's to keep you hanging around through the winter so that I can use you as a guide again in the spring.

"And you can't spend the money all on liquor," she added. "I need you to be in good shape. Next summer I want to go higher and back farther in the mountains."

Megan worked hard in her mine, and blasted carefully where the seam took her. Ore began to pile up, awaiting the spring thaw to take it out to the assayer's office. She talked to Newton when she was lonely, and he looked at her with velvet eyes, moving his big ears as if he understood. She kept the animal in a lean-to next to her cabin, with a door into her cabin so she didn't have to go outside to feed him when the snow came down in a frenzy, as it often did.

Each morning, Megan looked out over the vast mountain ranges while she walked to the mine. The unimpeded view of the mountains spreading across the top of the world almost made her weep with joy.

♔

When the snow had melted enough for Megan to go to town, she went to Homer's hotel.

The hotel proprietor cleared his throat and looked down, unwilling to bear bad news. "Homer's dead. He froze to death."

Megan felt as if the man had hit her. "What happened?"

"It had been snowing for two days, and the boardwalk was slippery. He was drunk for sure, and he fell in the alley just outside. I found him in the morning."

Shocked by her suddenly pale face and worried that she might faint, as women often did, he added, "It's supposed to be an easy death, freezing. You just fall asleep. He was smiling. You all right, Miss O'Sullivan?"

Megan was surprised at the tears that came suddenly to her eyes, and she blinked fast to hide her weakness. "The old fool!" she said. "Now what am I going to do?" She turned away and pretended to look out the window. Homer Beaufort had just been a crotchety old man, she told herself.

The hotel proprietor was speaking again. "I had him buried properly, and I asked the Baptist minister to say some words, since Homer had been a preacher himself once."

Megan paid the man for the coffin and Homer's gravesite and thanked him for his work. Then she went to the cemetery. She felt Homer needed some words from her, to make him rest easy.

"' . . . He maketh me to lie down in green pastures: he leadeth me beside the still waters. He restoreth my soul: he leadeth me in the paths of righteousness . . . '"

♛

Megan tramped for miles that late spring and summer, her brown hair tied back with a rawhide string, her hat tied firmly under her chin against the mountain winds. She staked more claims, doing the work necessary to prove each one with the help of muscular young men she hired in town.

She missed Homer Beaufort, that cussed, smelly old man.

Most of the men who followed Megan surreptitiously when she went looking for a new lode gave up when she went above the 14,000 foot level. They sat on the ground gasping for oxygen, complaining to each other about that uppity woman.

♛

After twenty years of doing this hard work and loving most of every minute, Megan realized her sight was dimming. She needed more and more candles in the mines to see even the brightest gold veins. She developed rheumatism in her back and her knees. Even having the young men to help wasn't enough. Megan was tired.

She took Newton's big head in her hands and brushed the gray hairs on his muzzle. "Well, old friend, you and I are getting a little rickety. Much as I hate to say it, these mountains are getting to be too much for us. What do you think? How about a nice warm stall full of hay down in town?" Newton nuzzled her pocket for the sugar lump he knew she had there.

Megan O'Sullivan's bank account had grown enough to call for respect in town. She told Mr. Gump, the bank president, she wanted to lease her mines. He knew some people (including himself) who might be interested. Megan drove a hard bargain, as usual, but eventually all of her holdings were leased.

The last time she looked out of her cabin up by the Megan Mine she couldn't see the roof of the world any more.

Megan walked down the mountain that last time with a fresh clean breeze on her face and her rheumatism forgotten. She led a drooping Newton loaded with the few items she thought she would keep, and she wondered what she would do in town among other women.

Megan realized how tired she was when she came to a little uphill stretch. Newton held back on the lead rope at this prospect, and Megan turned to look at him. In slow motion, the mule settled on his haunches and then, very finally, he lay down on his side and breathed out a great sigh.

This couldn't be! Newton was her only friend in the world! Megan begged the animal to get up. But it was no use.

She stood up, gasping a little at the pain in her joints.

Megan O'Sullivan walked down the trail alone, feeling as if a great weight was pressing down on her.

Once Megan turned and looked back for Newton, feeling strange to have no lead rope in her hand, his warm breath on her neck. Tears made rivulets in the dust on her face. But Megan brushed them off with her work-hardened hand and made herself think back on the good times. She walked until she could smell the smoke rising from the chimneys of the town and hear a horse whinnying. Her words were still firm as she recited scripture she had learned from Homer Beaufort long ago:

"'To every thing there is a season, and a time to every purpose under the heaven,

A time to be born, and a time to die; a time to plant, and a time to pluck up that which is planted . . . '" Megan's voice faltered as she searched for the words, and then she spoke out again. "'A time to weep, and a time to laugh; a time to mourn, and a time to dance . . . '"

Diary Fragments
Found in an Attic

Sherie Fox Schmauder

SIXTEEN
Diary Fragments Found in an Attic

April 12, 1874

Our house is on the hill above the mine, and Frederick had the men build a good stout stone wall in front of it, so the yard would be fairly level. The men built us a fine house, with an ell for the kitchen, to keep the summer heat from the rest of the house. The roof is peaked, but not so steep that it doesn't need help when the snow mounts higher and higher. If the winds don't come roaring up the valley and whirl it off, one of the men who worked on our house comes with a roof rake made like a gigantic comb with a long handle and encourages the snow to fall in great drifts.

♛

August 27, 1874

Frederick is always busy with the mine, spending all of his days while it is light in the peaked building that looks like a poor excuse for an Oriental pagoda. I sit on the screened porch the nice man from the mine, Mr. Wright, built for me. Frederick gives him a day off now and then from the mine to do things for me.

Otherwise, Mr. Wright is down in the deep roots of the ground, where it is always above freezing and well below comfort if you sit still. Of course the men never sit still, pounding and picking and dynamiting to coax the gold ore from its mother matrix, the solid rock, crushed by the weight of all that is above it, weighted by the tantalizing whisper of what still might be below.

♛

September 19, 1874

Ernest Wright, the very kind young man who has done chores for me, went down to Central City and brought me small lilac bushes, which he said had belonged to a lady who had given up and gone back East to her mother. Her man had been killed in a cave-in.

There are always cave-ins in the mines, and always crushed bodies being brought to the surface after they are mined themselves from the heartless rubble that buries them. Although there are some ore seams that peter out once they have eaten the flesh of the miners, no one will leave a comrade there in a lightless grave—not if there is a chance of lifting his mangled remains up to the clear air above. They all want to be buried just six feet below friendly soil, not deep within unyielding rock.

♛

June 3, 1875

Last fall, Ernest planted the lilac bushes for me above the rock walls that rim my front lawn. He cut the grass with a scythe after the glorious riot of summer flowers had faded and the air turned crisp in mid-day. The winter was not so hard this year. The bushes thrived and have just flowered.

Frederick comes in at night bone tired from urging his men onward and downward. The pile of gold that is his share after he pays his partners grows in the bank in Central City (the one that survived the dreadful fire). He told me to go in the buggy and buy myself clothes to make me look the fine young lady I was when he met me and my parents down in Denver.

I laughed at that. What am I to do with fancy clothing way up here on the mountain in my house with the small lilac bushes in the dooryard? I pour my husband a hot bath and let him soak the dirt and dust from his body, but it can't soak away his thoughts of the wealth we will have some day. He says he will find the mother lode, the vein that will make Eldorado look a poor cousin. We both like that idea.

Each morning at daybreak after a nourishing breakfast of ham and eggs and fried potatoes with gravy, he leaves the house. In winter I kiss him goodbye before the sun lightens the sky. At night he sits over his figures. Sometimes the comforting rumble of his talk with the foremen in the parlor lulls me to insensible sleep. Eventually he joins me, fits himself to my back awkwardly. In his sleep, he mumbles of the riches just around the bend in the next tunnel.

✠

June 19, 1875

Ernie has planted my garden of potatoes and carrots, cabbages, beans and onions. I bought the rich dresses and wear them while we sit on the screened porch Ernie built for me. We drink cold tea from crystal glasses my parents sent, and exclaim how high the lilac bushes have grown. Ernie and I talk of Denver, and of the East, and of the riches that are Europe. It is enjoyable to sit there with him.

When Frederick comes home for supper he sometimes walks to his desk, commenting on how the smell of lilacs permeates our small house, and his smile flickers at me in my finery as I wait at the table for him to join me. But the chicken cools and the tea becomes tepid while he scratches down figures in his big ledger. I finally wait for him out in the dark of my screened porch. We chat before we go to bed.

✠

May 7, 1876

I could not write of this until now. One morning last fall the mine whistle shrieked. I flew out of my small house, through my screened porch, past my growing lilac bushes and down to the mine with all the other wives. The crew had only been below ground for part of the morning. We waited outside the tall mine shaft building for news of which tunnel, how deep, who was working there, what had happened...

Had Frederick been below discussing a new vein with the foremen? Who else had been in that tunnel? I shook, and my mouth was dry. Other women were crying already.

At last the elevator cage came up. Survivors! The ambulance cart carried away the moaning, the maimed, the mutilated. Still not the one I waited to find. I grew dizzy with holding my breath.

The knot of wives grew smaller. We stood with white faces, clutching black shawls over our heads in the wan light of the cloudy September day. The wind rose as it always does in mid-day, whipping the dust and dirt around us, turning us gray and haggard.

The shaft elevator creaked to life again and rose from the pit. Did spirits rise too? Two covered forms lay on canvas stretchers. Frederick hunched between the two, his hands bleeding. He must have been trying to dig them out. But who were they? Slowly the men lifted the still forms out of the elevator. They trudged with them to the ambulance wagon. The mule team looked back, flicked their ears nervously and stamped their hooves. The other wife left with me looked under one tarpaulin and wailed, her voice echoing down the canyon.

Frederick saw me and turned. He gestured to the other mound of canvas.

"He was a fine young man, and as earnest a worker as his name. He has no people," Frederick said. "Could you bear to see to the poor lad and prepare him for burial?"

I felt I would fall then, but I could not let my husband see such emotion over a mere miner, even one who had done chores for me. With a great effort of will, I remained standing, though I turned away so he could not see my face. I hoped he would think it was the dust-blown wind in my eyes. "Yes, of course," I managed to say.

I sprinkled heart-shaped lilac leaves on his grave that day. Now that it is spring again I have planted one of my small flowering bushes over his heart.

Quaking Aspens

Sherie Fox Schmauder

SEVENTEEN
Quaking Aspens

*V*erity Messenger sat rigidly beside her husband on the wagon seat, fighting the rocking and lurching of the wagon. Once again, she quelled visions of her belongings coming loose; her china, her books, her clothing, everything she owned crashing on to the dirt road, broken and shredded. She shifted uncomfortably. By this stage of their everlasting journey, she was bruised and sore, her mind reduced to smoking rubble.

Tad had insisted this was the way to travel. He had said they would appreciate the distance and beauties of the land more if they came by wagon, instead of taking the train part way. There had been rumors of a railroad making its way to Aspen, but that was years away. The only thing this interminable trip had accomplished was to make her yearn for the life she'd left behind.

She knew she would never have a home again, she'd live among Indians and dirty ignorant miners. She hadn't spoken to Tad for two days. Even her own parents had not been sympathetic to her wish to stay in Kansas. Verity felt like a leaf tossed aimlessly on the wind, with no mind of her own. How could she have stayed when her own family told her she must go with her husband?

She thought, *I gave up my family and civilization to be with Tad, so he could set up a business that I loathe with all of my being. How could he decide on such a profession after I had already committed my life to his? Even in a city back East, I'd hate to be an undertaker's wife. I will hate this land forever.*

♛

Aspen was in a lovely valley, Verity had to admit. After settling in their house, she found nothing to do except dust her belongings, read her books over and over, and write longing letters back home. There was no social life. Tad was gone all day, except for lunch, setting up his new undertaking business next door. As bored as she was, she would have nothing to do with that. Tad had tried hard to get her involved, suggesting she play the little pedal organ for the funerals.

They had argued about his work. Tad was adamant. What started it all was that fiasco at his father's funeral. The improperly constructed casket had fallen out of the pallbearers' hands and spilled the body, which had rolled with a horrifying, ungainly motion into the opened grave. Tad's mother had fainted, and Tad found a new profession. Tad wanted to make sure no other family was ever put through such a shocking experience. Not if he could help it.

In Aspen, Tad ordered the best coffins from Denver for those who could afford it, and he had a local carpenter make sturdy pine boxes for those who could not.

There were many funerals, but the saddest ones were for children. There were plenty of those. Children died from any number of reasons here in this primitive, cold area. Some came from rich families, some came from poor ones. Some were unwanted, and had been treated poorly. Some came from nowhere.

The bodies of unwanted infants began appearing on Verity's back doorstep soon after they had moved in. Some of the tiny creatures looked like babies, but premature, while others were just sacs of fluid with vague forms inside. Miscarriages or secret abortions?

Verity was revolted. She began having nightmares about the infants. Why leave them at her house instead of at the funeral home next door? Even Tad's face blanched when he saw that first baby. Obviously dead hours ago. Probably never opened its eyes. Premature, it fit in the palm of Tad's capable hand and was wrapped in a pink silk scrap, most likely from a fancy woman's skirt.

After the sixth baby, Verity began to take it personally. Why were these women doing this to her? She had nothing to do with their lives. True, she was courteous when she met them on the wooden sidewalk, where they promenaded with their gaudy clothes and their ruffled sunshades, but they had nothing in common at all.

Except the babies?

She supposed that these women had found some way to miscarry or otherwise get rid of the bits of humanity that would threaten their money-making ability.

Verity tried to think of what the prostitutes' lives must be like. She couldn't imagine there could be any real love in their coupling for money, nothing lasting. What kind of life would a child born in a brothel have, anyway? Still, it was sad. What did the women think when they lost their babies?

Well, that was no business of hers, Verity decided. She would never have children, not in a place like Aspen. Not until she could give them the advantages of civilization. Would she ever be able to leave this place where dead babies appeared on her doorstep almost daily?

Verity began to anticipate her morning "gift." She learned to look down on her back porch floor every morning before she stepped out. She would call Tad, and he would come take the wrapped infant away. She would scrub the porch then, though there was never any sign of what had been there. The bundles were always carefully wrapped in a bit of finery.

Tad buried the tiny beings among the aspens in a large grove outside of town. The babies shouldn't be in the town cemetery, he said, with all that human agony there. The aspen grove was peaceful, and the trees whispered to each other all day and night. They would sing to the infants and comfort them. Verity liked that idea.

One day as Tad was driving Verity to nearby Ashcroft to visit a friend, Verity thought she saw a dark form slipping among the white trees where the babies slept. Perhaps a bereft mother? Tad had put little white wooden crosses at the head of each infant, with the date it had been found, and the sex, if he could tell.

If I were one of those women, Verity mused as the carriage rattled along, *would I pray at the grave of my baby if I had been forced to get rid of it? I can't imagine the agony of losing a child, but yes, I would do just that. I would pray for forgiveness, to bless my baby, to talk to it and try to make it understand how hard it is to live on earth.*

Those poor women.

Tad's work brought dignity to the sad deaths of these infants. At last Verity relented and realized the good of his chosen profession. She smiled to herself as the sunlight flickered through the aspen trees.

One snowy morning when Verity looked out her back door just at daybreak, another bundle was lying in a box. And it was moving.

Verity froze for a moment. She flung open the door and scooped up the tiny baby. Out of the corner of her eye she saw a flurry of movement, but when she looked closer, a squall of snow obscured her view.

Back inside her warm kitchen, where the lamp on the table cast a glow and the big iron stove radiated heat, she laid the infant on the table. She hastily unwrapped the white silk. A small boy, umbilical cord tied. He was blue, and cold to the touch, but still, he moved.

Verity might shudder to bring a new child into this place peopled with losers, liars, dreamers, men who only wanted to dig in the dirt, and women whose only currency was their bodies. But she could not allow this little boy to die. She picked up the child and undid the buttons of her bodice. Nestling him against her skin, she felt him slowly warm, his soft breath against her breast, searching. She would need some way to feed him.

She smiled and the frozen bowl of her many losses that year shattered. She called to Tad, joy in her voice. He came running out of the bedroom, bumping into the door jamb in his waking confusion.

Quick! He must go to a family with babies, find a nursing mother. No argument, he must go now. This baby needed food. He looked at Verity and smiled, seeing that she was happy at last. The child was a gift from heaven. He slammed the door on his hasty way out, half dressed, slipping on the new snow.

Verity hoped the baby's mother could rest tonight, knowing, at least this time, her baby would be in loving arms and not beneath an aspen tree. Perhaps coming to Aspen had been a good idea after all. This baby made it all worth while.

Some Things the Ore Carts Carry

EIGHTEEN
Some Things the Ore Carts Carry

*T*he ore cart sits now in the meadow, giving no intimation of the sad freight it once held. One day our Timmy, three years old, a child with violent tempers, sneaked from the house to the mineshaft, while I was bent over the wash tub.

Forbidden to go near the mine, the boy willfully went to the opening, stowed his small self in an ore cart, and managed to release the hand brake. He rumbled down the shaft hidden under a gunnysack.

Just as ore was being dumped into the cart at the working end of the tunnel, Horace Appleton, the foreman, saw Timmy's little blond head and snatched him out by a handful of hair. Not quick enough to stop the cascading rocks from breaking Timmy's leg.

Ethan had beaten Timmy after he had nearly fallen into a disused shaft earlier that spring, but the child merely laughed, feeling no pain. The tunnels drew him like an addict to opium. I had latched the screen door high above his reach, but he'd learned to drag a chair very quietly to the door. I had always managed to catch him as he flew across the meadow toward the shaft.

Until that day.

Ethan nailed boards around the child's trundle bed and put a heavy screen over the top, making a cage under the window where the boy could look out, though he shrieked and wailed and said words I thought no three-year-old would know. He was to stay there while his leg healed and his father worked. Timmy became so violent at being locked in this pen that he damaged himself, butting his head at the boards and ripping off his splint. I could not leave him for a minute. I found my chores impossible to complete before Ethan came home for supper.

One day Timmy bashed his head with a particularly powerful thrust against his prison wall. He fell senseless onto the mattress. I cried out to him, and tore off the screen top.

Trembling, I felt for his heartbeat. It was strong, but too fast. I ran for help.

The mine doctor feared for his life. But some days later my little blond angel woke up and smiled. Ever since then, my sweet Timmy sits wherever he is placed; cheerful and sunny-faced, his speech lost. He plays with stones and string, the youngest victim of the Baldwin Mine.

Ethan still loved the deep mine, the dark tunnels, the screeching ore carts. He scorned to notice his son any more, and came to blame me for Timmy's condition. One day he moved on to fresher diggings, feeling the guilt of having such a child, I suppose. I do not mind his loss.

Now my Timmy and I live alone in our small house. Below us, at the bottom of the meadow, is all that is left of the mine that took our future.

Horace Appleton brings me groceries from Gunnison, and he is kind. Sometimes he brings toys to Timmy, and I like the way he plays with the boy. Horace has asked me to go with him to Gunnison, to bring Timmy where there are other children. But I cannot imagine leaving this beautiful valley yet, though I know death still lurks hidden underground. I still hope the calm and beauty of the place will bring light to Timmy's mind one day.

Timmy has learned to let me hug him, and some day perhaps he will see me again when he looks at me.

Every spring I take him with me to the boarded entrance to the mine.

Together we plant morning glories there, and around the one remaining ore cart that was left to rot nearby. By the end of summer the mine entry and the cart are hidden.

But they never disappear from our lives.

Independence

Sherie Fox Schmauder

NINETEEN
Independence

"*D*o you love me? You'll never leave me, will you?" Kate woke hearing those hated words again and sat bolt upright in her little cabin next to the log schoolhouse. Her breath was frozen in the air as she gasped, her heart racing, and before she was entirely awake she was searching the room for William, an automatic prayer on her lips it would not be so.

Nor was it. William was moldering in his grave. She had left Philadelphia in a frantic hurry, before he rose out of his coffin to keep her there in that airless house under his mother's watchful eyes.

She had not seen the signs of his insanity when William courted her. He had been a consummate actor. Kate thanked God that he had died.

William had become more unhinged mentally as his disease progressed. He thought if Kate left his side he would die. He had clutched at her with emaciated hands.

Of course he was going to die; he had consumption! The fear that she would catch the dreaded disease had led Kate to wash her hands compulsively, had made her open the window whenever he finally dozed off to sleep. She kept a handkerchief tied over her nose and mouth. But she also had to cope with William's mother, herself burning with the disease but still upright as long as she thought she could will her son to life. Near the end, Mrs. Gordon had decided that if it took chaining Kate to William's bedstead to keep him alive, Kate would be chained.

❧

Mrs. Gordon had kept Kate a prisoner all the time, except when the undertaker came to prepare William for burial and people came with condolences. Mrs. Gordan told Kate she would keep her chained as punishment for allowing William to die. Kate finally escaped, with the help of her friend Hermione, whose brother had told her how to pick the chain lock. While

Kate's mother-in-law visited a friend for the afternoon, she slipped out of the house with her belongings.

Kate swore Hermione to secrecy as she embarked on the train heading for Denver. She was going to a mining town high in the Colorado Rockies. Mrs. Gordon would not wish to follow her, even if she knew her destination.

Independence had advertised in the eastern papers for a teacher, and Kate had secretly answered the ad. She liked the name "Independence," even though the place was mountainous and cold. She had played up her abilities a bit perhaps, but how hard could it be to teach a roomful of children?

And now she quailed before the prospect. The only children she had seen on the dirt street yesterday, when she arrived, had been wild, poorly dressed, and shrill voiced.

Today was her first day of school. She rose, shivering. (But it was only the first of September! Surely those were not snowflakes dusting the windowsill?) Thank heavens she'd bought warm woolen underclothing in Denver.

Out on the street, wrapped in her sturdy black wool cape, clutching a heavy bag of books and papers, Kate passed a line of hard-looking men. They had dirt ingrained in the pores of their faces, and helmets with candles set in the front. Miners. They looked at her with interest. She held her head high, trying to look efficient and strong. Her 5'10" height alone helped the effort. She wanted nothing at all to do with men, not ever again.

"Beg pardon, Ma'am, but would you be the new school teacher?" Wearing a heavy black work coat and grimy dark blue denim pants, the man met Kate eye to eye. He was stocky, and presented a rock solid appearance, something like a sturdy building. His look was penetrating, and Kate moved back a step. But he was courteous, and he tipped his hat. The men with him were silent, listening.

"Yes, I would be the new school teacher, Mr . . . .?" she returned calmly. She thought he might have children in school.

"Wester, Luke Wester. I'm the foreman for the Crazy Burro Mine. I'd be pleased to show you the town after my shift, Ma'am. I could carry firewood, or do some heavy chores."

"Thank you, but I fear I shall be swamped with homework after meeting my pupils. They will help me with firewood. Will I have one of your children in class?"

The man laughed and looked down, scuffed his feet almost bashfully, and several miners joined in his laughter.

"Not likely, Ma'am, at least none I recognize."

Kate looked away from this looming man. None that he recognized?

Across the rutted street, a tall, Lincolnesque man stood with one foot off the board sidewalk as if to cross the street toward her, a smile on his face. He was untidy, his coat flapping in the wind. Was she to be inundated with men hoping for her acquaintance? She wanted nothing to do with men!

Kate dismissed Mr. Wester, swept past the miners and went into the school building. As she closed the door, she saw the other man continuing his walk in the other direction. Who was he? She frowned. Never mind.

♕

Kate's first day of class was a mixed success. She could not let up her control for a minute, especially with the older boys. The little ones obviously had learned no discipline either. The week flew by. By Friday, she wondered why she had ever thought teaching children would be easy.

She stuck with it, though, and soon she began to see progress. A few of the first graders overcame their reluctance to learn their ABCs and laboriously made unsteady letters on their slates, tongues stuck out to aid in concentration. Smiles illuminated their faces when she praised them.

The older children recognized her command of the material and fell more or less in line, except for the big boys. They discovered Kate's discomfort at the nearness of small many-legged creatures, though she tried hard to control it. Finally she managed to make a joke of her squeamishness, and then gave them a science lesson on spiders. With that, she won them.

If some of them did poorly in school again this year, they would be yanked into the mines to work beside their fathers. She did not want to let that happen.

Edwin Whitacker, a thirteen-year-old, was a worse problem than the pranksters. He had been stuck for years in the fourth grade, according to the last teacher's records, because he couldn't learn to write a proper sentence in a forward manner, nor could he tell the difference between "God" and "dog." His letters were more frequently backward than frontward.

Kate made him her special project. She would not let him go into the mines. She made him stay after school several afternoons, which seemed to do some good. Edwin seemed to be memorizing the letter shapes, and he tried hard.

Her life was not calm outside of the classroom. If she was out of her cabin when the mine shifts changed, Luke Wester managed to find her. The children's mothers had told her about him, saying they had heard rumors of his behavior in the saloons. Yet he did go to church whenever the traveling preacher appeared. Kate saw that the miners worshipped him, and she had been told he had rescued several men when a tunnel had collapsed.

One windy day at dusk Kate was on her way home with groceries. A strong gust nearly unbalanced her, and she dropped her bag. Before she could pick up the tins of peaches and the oatmeal box, Wester was helping her. He put his hand on her arm and propelled her to her little cabin. Before she could enter and shut him out, he was inside, putting the burlap grocery bag on the book-littered table.

He wore a cleaner coat than he had before, and his face was red from the wind. He took off his knit cap, revealing tousled black hair. He turned to her, with a hesitant manner, his dark eyes focused on her face.

"I know you are a woman of the world, Miss Gordon, and I know you came here for a reason of your own. But I also know you need someone to take care of you. You don't know how lonely and hard it can be in mid-winter." He looked at the piles of books on the table. "I want to take care of you. I have a big cabin, enough room for both of us. I want to marry you."

Kate was totally shocked! Marry him? She barely knew him! She would never marry again. She realized he was still speaking, though she hadn't heard his words.

" . . . You wouldn't need to teach any more, or take more sass from those young whippersnappers. I heard about them putting spiders and such in your desk drawer." He grinned then, looking boyish himself. "I hope I haven't made a bad impression somehow. It's been a long time since I've met a real lady."

Shocked at the man's temerity and frightened at his nearness, Kate stood open-mouthed and speechless. Then the memory of her prior life came back. She clenched her teeth, and then managed to speak.

"You are presuming far too much, Mr. Wester," she said. "I have no desire to marry. And I love those 'whippersnappers!' I thank you for helping me with my groceries, but you are not welcome in my home. Please leave."

They stared at one another, she glaring, he shocked that she was so upset. He dropped his eyes first, with an apologetic look.

"I'm sorry. I seem to have jumped the gun. I should have given you a chance to know me better," he said. He turned abruptly and went to the door. "Ask any of the men. I'm not a bad person. Sounds like you've been mistreated by someone. Perhaps I could buy you dinner at the café sometime." Luke Wester put on his cap and let himself out the door.

♔

Determined to prove Mr. Luke Wester wrong about her loneliness, Kate made an effort to make more friends. She worked on the church bazaar. Then she decided she would write educational articles for the local paper.

Still idealistic about the idea of educating the children to the outside world, she decided to write about the culture of the East; about concerts, libraries, commerce, great schools. She could help boys see they didn't need to enter the mine at twelve.

The girls needn't become downtrodden housewives. They could learn to make their own way in this world.

Pleased with her first little article, about life in Philadelphia, Kate marched resolutely to the door of the *Independence Leader*. She had admired the low-key, well-written articles she had read in the paper. The editor must be a man of learning and refinement.

A bell over the door jingled when she entered. The small room held a wooden counter littered with papers and a roll-top desk weighed down by stacks of more papers. The smell of printer's ink permeated the air. From another room, behind a dirty curtain, came the sounds of banging metal and someone cursing.

The man who had met her eyes from across the street that early September day strode into the room. He wore a rubber apron and his hands were black and greasy with ink.

"May I speak to the editor, please?" she said firmly, refusing to meet his look any longer than necessary. The cursing in the next room lapsed into incoherent mutterings.

"I am the editor and owner, Ma'am. Jason Tudor. How may I be of service?"

Kate introduced herself, though in such a small town as this he undoubtedly already knew who she was. She explained her mission, her grand goal of educating the populace to the glories of the outside world. She thrust her pages toward him, suddenly afraid her writing was not good.

He scanned it rapidly, his pencil making illegible markings in the margin. He cleared his throat. "I like this part very much, about what the city looks like; this next part, well, maybe not. I wonder if what you write about the shops and the goods available, the food choices, might make the women homesick and dissatisfied with their lot here." He looked at the dismay in her face. "Though I'm sure this was not what you intended, Miss Gordon."

His blue eyes pierced her failing composure. Still, he had meant his comments to be helpful. Kate wanted to go out and hide under the boardwalk, but she could see the value in his words. She took back the now grubby pages of her article.

He saw her confusion. "Miss Gordon, why don't you start with short pieces on how to help children learn in school. Coming from an expert such as yourself, your words would surely be welcomed by parents."

Just then, a cry and a crash came from the printing room. Jason Tudor disappeared through the curtain. Alarmed, Kate sped after him.

A small, weak-chinned young man was sitting on the floor sobbing, obviously drunk. Bits of metal type lay all around him, and he held a large empty metal tray.

"You idiot," Tudor roared. "That's the whole front page you just dumped! You're fired!" He ran his inky hand through his brown hair and stood glowering while the man scrambled unsteadily to his feet and went careening through the curtain. The jangling bell marked his uncertain passage out the door, and a blast of cold air told Kate he had not shut it after himself. Silently, she went to do so.

When she returned to the printing room, Jason Tudor was on his knees doggedly placing the small metal letters into a long, narrow metal box he held in one hand. He looked up at her entry. "I'm sorry, Miss Gordon. As you see . . . "

"I can help you, Mr. Tudor. I'll put on this apron" (she grimaced distastefully as she took down a dirty rubberized apron) "and you can tell me what to do. Do you have another of those boxes?"

He looked up at her and relaxed for a moment. He smiled. "Composing stick. One on that table over there. You'll get dirty, Miss Gordon. But you are very kind. Paper copy for this particular story," and here he pushed a pile of type toward her, "is on that spindle. Headline reads 'Collapse in Farwell Mine Kills Two.'"

It took some doing for Kate to figure out how to read the words backwards, as that was how the type letters had to be set, but before long she settled into a rhythm. She forgot her dirty hands, intent on learning this new craft, if only for today.

It was dark and cold when the two left the office, and Tudor walked her the short way to her cabin. As they stood on her doorstep, she offered to help find him a new apprentice. He smiled at the improbability of such a thing. "That won't be easy."

But an idea had come to Kate as the wind whipped her shawl around her and tugged at her bonnet. "One of my schoolboys has been unable to learn to read properly. He gets his letters and words backwards. You set type in the same manner."

Jason Tudor seemed pleased with the idea. He walked away quickly after pressing Kate's gloved hand with his own. As she went inside, she frowned, uneasy at her response to this man.

Monday morning when Kate set out for school, heavily bundled in layers of wool that did nothing to keep out the rising icy wind, she looked at lowering clouds scud overhead. The peaks of Independence Pass were already invisible. She sighed. How long could she live where snow came so early and so high?

The icy wind brought a blizzard. By the time Kate realized how dark the room had become, even with the hanging lanterns, it was too late to send the children home without adult escorts. No recess, of course, and they would eat their lunches drawn up close to the potbellied stove. Luckily the woodbin was well stocked.

They could see no other buildings from the windows through the driving snow. The smaller children looked frightened as the wind moaned and battered the log walls, worming its way through chinks and even swirling papers about Kate's desk. Everyone wore coats.

Grades seven and eight had been studying government, so Kate held a mock election. Soon she had a Supreme Court, a small Senate, and Representatives. The voting made Kate President, while Edwin, who had been the spirited leader of the election, became Vice-President. Kate led a rousing series of songs after the children had eaten, and made them all march around the room until they were finally cheered and warm.

After the excitement died down, Kate read some fairy tales. But then a couple of younger children began to cry. As she comforted them on her lap, Kate feared they all would have to spend the night — would the firewood hold out? Would she?

A thumping at the front door, accompanied by a snowy whirl of wind as the door opened, announced the arrival of miners looking for their children. The crews had been pulled out early, knowing it would be difficult to make it out later.

"We had to fight our way to the schoolhouse," one man said, his happy eight-year-old in his arms.

Another added, "It would be foolhardy to take the smaller children out in this blizzard. The wind is too strong. In the morning it'll probably clear, and we can shovel our way home. Everyone in town will be shoveling, soon as the wind dies down."

A third man spoke up. "We'll shelter here for the night. We'll be fine."

"What about your wives and babies?" Kate asked.

"No help for it. This has happened before. Everyone knows to leave goodly supplies of wood in the house, every day. Our women are used to making do on their own. Neighbors will look in on them."

Dear God, those poor women with their babies! Kate's face was grim.

A few men who had older children and lived close by set out for their homes. Before the door closed on them, Luke Wester came in. He automatically began taking control.

Kate felt a strange relief at his competence, but was determined to rule her own school. "The children would be happier to have no more disruption Mr. Wester. You're welcome to stay and help, but that is all." She knew if she lost control to Luke Wester, her authority would go down in the children's eyes.

Edwin stood up. Not quite knowing what to do with his hands, he looked Wester in the eyes and said, "You can't boss Miss Gordon, Mr. Wester. We just elected her President of this United States schoolhouse, and anyway, she's the teacher and when you're here you have to do what she says."

Wester raised his eyebrows. The other men chuckled, turning aside so he couldn't see how tickled they were at this young sprout. Edwin glanced nervously at the teacher. The kid obviously had a crush on her.

Wester smiled and apologized for his presumption. He chatted with one of the men.

He had never been obnoxious, thought Kate. After all, only the one intrusion and his demand for something she could not give. He was a leader of men; that must say something for his character. He was a kind man, she knew, and now he turned to cheer up a young boy whose father had not come to the schoolhouse.

More sounds of arrival, and several merchants came in, stamping off the snow in the coatroom, putting heavy boxes of groceries and blankets into willing arms. Last to enter was Jason Tabor. He had gone blindly from building to building, almost by touch, Kate was told, alerting the merchants to the probable situation in the schoolhouse. His laboriously re-created newspaper edition was forgotten.

Kate realized this was what a community was all about: sticking together, doing for one another. Children were the most important commodity here, and the people had come to save them. She would pray the isolated mothers with tiny children would be all right. Neighbors surely would look in on them. She smiled at the busy, happy children rooting through food boxes, sitting on fathers' laps, whispering to best friends.

Jason Tabor watched her, and she looked into his blue eyes. He seemed poised to come to her side should she need him.

Then she glanced at Luke Wester, and saw a strange expression come over his face as he watched Jason Tabor hand an apple to a child. Wester turned away with apparent effort.

She imagined a disturbing current in the air between the two men, and knew she was the reason. Sitting at her desk with a sleepy six-year-old sucking his thumb on her lap, Kate decided she needed to sort out the disturbing currents running through her own life before she could concentrate on these two men she barely knew.

Perhaps it was the air of these Rocky Mountains that made her able to look within herself with more clarity. She liked her independence, and she would never allow it to be taken away. For now, her students had her heart. One day, there would be room for more.

The Bob & Wave

TWENTY
The Bob & Wave

*M*yrna remembered her panic at that earthquake she'd felt on her sweet sixteenth birthday in Missouri, when she was a skinny, dishwater blonde with no sex appeal whatsoever. Now she wondered why she stayed here in Victor, Colorado, with its miles of mines beneath the streets, and every so often an explosion shivering the ground, sending her antennae fluttering helplessly and she having to make excuses for jerking someone's hair or glopping wave lotion over the cape tied around the woman's shoulders.

Well, she knew for sure why she was here in Victor: it was the last place Lance Vaduz, that jail-bird liar con-man would ever think to look for her. He'd been an earthquake in her life, taking her out of Missouri the next year when she was a mere sweet seventeen and never been kissed, except by him. Myrna owed that to Aunt Carlie, who'd given her a bleach job and some good make-up (and my, hadn't Mama screeched!). Lance Vaduz had changed her life, for sure.

Then he'd gotten himself put in jail in Denver — imagine! She'd been so dumb she never realized all those "withdrawals" he made at banks while she waited in the car were really robberies. His drinking had been bad enough, not as bad as her father's, to be sure. But robbery? Myrna had been terrified of being put in jail.

The Denver police had been on to him, but she'd been able to get out of the hotel by the skin of her teeth, while Lance Valduz raced out another hotel door into their arms, not hers. Myrna's clothes had been spilling out of her cardboard suitcase as she tried to walk sedately out the door, the small canvas bag of stolen money banging on her thighs where she'd pinned it under her dress. The money had been enough to get her to Victor and then some.

When she had felt the first tremor from the mines below, she'd nearly gone into a heart attack. Yes she had. It had been a real chore to make herself stay here in The Bob & Wave Salon, gritting her teeth and trying not to jump every time the lotion and shampoo bottles on the shelves jittered and skittered about. Even railings meant to stop them from flying off into the air and down on the floor sometimes didn't work.

Sort of like Myrna felt most of the time, as if she was about to fly into the air, though she thought she'd done a pretty good job hiding her fear of both the mine quakes and Lance Vaduz. She didn't know how long he was in jail for. She hadn't taken very much money from his big gladstone bag, which had been crammed full of more money than she ever knew existed. Maybe he wouldn't come after her.

Anyway, now she didn't look like the old Myrna, and there were plenty of other Myrnas if he heard the name, so he shouldn't home in on this place. Nothing in Victor anyway, except the mines and the hookers and the saloons and other women trying desperately to be ladies while their men toiled under the ground like moles. Maybe Lance'd go to Cripple Creek, where there was more action and bigger mines. And probably prettier prostitutes than the ones in Victor. Myrna avoided Cripple Creek, just in case.

She had beautiful platinum blonde hair now, with perfect marcelled waves. Her eyebrows were plucked so they made her look wide awake. Her long nails were lacquered a bright red. Her skirts were shorter, her knees rouged like a flapper's should be, and she could go for weeks without running her silk stockings if she remembered to wear gloves to put them on. Myrna privately thought she looked like the cat's meow.

Yes, her life had taken a turn for the better, especially since she had met Rod Casey. Oh yes, Myrna knew he kept coming into The Bob & Wave because she was the only woman who had turned him down. He wanted her to see the women flutter and primp and hide themselves from him when they were all dripping hair and dye covered, or attached to the octopus perm machine that clutched their hair in hot tight grips. At least he never got past the desk to harass any of the girls, including

Myrna, Mavis made sure of that. She ran a tight establishment, all proper.

Turning Rod Casey away had been no easy thing to do, he was so magnetic. He'd had his way with most of the women in Victor. Myrna had been the only one to run for her life. The man drank too much and that's what made her walk away. Not after Lance, and her father. She knew all about drinking.

But Rod Casey had a golden tongue, had probably kissed the Blarney Stone, so he said. When he spoke and told his stories it struck every woman in sight dumb, unable to move or breathe, numb with wonder, then electrically charged like a wayward perm machine. Myrna knew Rod would stick up for her if Lance Vaduz ever showed that chiseled face of his, with the curling black hair that she'd loved to twine in her hands.

Yes, fiery-haired Rod had muscles to spare from his work in the mines, and he would take Lance Vaduz apart limb by limb if he came to bother Myrna — even if Rod was seeing the Glory Mine owner's new wife on the side now.

Everyone had their secrets, and Myrna thought she knew most of the ones in Victor. It was shocking what a woman would tell a hairdresser as she sat in the chair, covered up in the big flowered cape, hair drifting down on it as Myrna cut and snipped and shaped. The chairs were far enough apart so that if you took the last one it would be hard for someone coming in to see who was being trimmed and marcelled and permed back there. That was the chair Myrna had claimed for her station, so she could slip out the back if she ever saw Lance Vaduz outside.

This Saturday morning Rod Casey did it again, carrying a big box that had come in the mail for the salon, probably that new wave lotion they'd ordered. Little Mr. Henry Hunt scurried along beside him, he being the mailman and not allowed to let the package out of his sight until Mavis had it, while Rod kept saying it was too heavy for Mr. Hunt, and couldn't he carry it inside The Bob & Wave?

Myrna yearned for Rod Casey like a dull gray moth to the burning lantern, but no, she wouldn't be fried, not she. Just then an underground explosion rumbled, and her world rocked around her — this one was much closer than they'd been this last week. She told herself it really had nothing to do with Rod Casey walking into The Bob & Wave. Her heart raced and her mouth felt dry. She was shaking. Every time there was a mine blast now she remembered the time a few weeks ago when a big hole had actually appeared in the middle of the street above a mine shaft. She clutched the back of the chair and said nothing.

Casey stood chatting with Mavis, his biceps rippling as he set the box on the counter. Mr. Henry Hunt went back out the door on his rounds. Everyone was silent. No one moved, the beauticians' hands poised to cut or curl or wash. Clients looked glassy-eyed at their own mirror reflections. Each woman strained to hear Rod Casey's melodious voice over the roar of the beehive dryer under which old Mrs. Wilson sat, oblivious to the tension in the shop, calmly reading her Ladies' Home Journal. Casey was telling Mavis about his big win at the Fortune Club last night. Mavis was probably the only one in the shop not smitten by him. She thought her own husband, the mine foreman, was twice the man Rod Casey was. No one else in the shop believed that.

Mrs. Clarissa Masters was sitting in Myrna's chair, and Myrna had just about finished a beautiful marcel job on her fine brown hair. Both of them had gone still and silent with the rest of the women listening to the golden voice of Rod Casey, when the door slammed open and in walked Mr. Masters himself, the big boss of the Glory Mine and new husband to Clarissa Masters. He waved a letter in one hand and spun Rod Casey around with the other, and though Rod put up his fists to pro-tect himself he hesitated. Myrna knew he'd be out of a job if he hit the owner of the Glory Mine.

"Do you know what's in this letter, Casey?" Masters roared in a tone guaranteed to be heard over Mrs. Wilson's dryer and clear down the street to the Fortune Club.

Rod Casey could see the handwriting on the wall if not in the letter, Myrna realized. She thought Clarissa Masters had stopped breathing, though she hadn't yet keeled over for lack of air. Casey began speaking in a quiet tone. No one could hear what he said, because of Mrs. Wilson's hairdryer. But they could all see the punch Mr. Masters landed on Casey's chin.

Myrna was frantic. She jerked to life and dropped her comb. She whirled around. Her careful life of obscurity would be shattered if there was mayhem and blood and The Bob & Wave became a headline story!

She ran through the shop, thrown slightly off her trajectory by another underground blast, but she kept on going.

"No, sir," she exclaimed, ignoring the drowning cry inside her, "whatever someone has told you it isn't true. He's my man, no one else's. He never looked at your pretty little wife — she's no match for a man like him." She stepped between the two men, who still had their fists up. "She needs the brains you got, not his muscles and his empty head, all this guy wants is sex," (collective gasp from the audience) "and that letter's just a jealous rumor . . . "

And all the time talking, standing in front of Rod Casey so Mr. Masters wouldn't hit him again, and there would be no newspaper story. Her mind and her mouth going a mile a minute. She was so close to Rod Casey that the fire of his body was consuming her. Myrna desperately did not want to be part of his life, but yet she did.

The room was still. Mrs. Wilson had turned off her hair dryer.

What had she done? Would she have to walk out of The Bob & Wave and the town of Victor to get clear of this man, like she had with Lance Valduz? Did she want to?

Should she quit running?

My List of Good Things

TWENTY-ONE
My List of Good Things

May 17, 1892

It's a real trial when this tent of ours blows down so frequently, yet if the wind, which comes from the snowfields, didn't blow, we wouldn't have clean air. The wind blows away all the dust from the placer mining that is so close to the village. Anyway, when the tent blows down, I reorganize things on the platform, and I get rid of the spiders that have been hiding in the corners.

June 2, 1892

Those snowfields above us decided to melt and come down in a big hurry this week. The river flooded, leaving the whole town a real mess. We were lucky, because our tent didn't come down. The dirty water with branches and even small dead animals flowed in one end and out the other, because Artemus thought fast enough to raise the canvas walls. We piled everything on top of the beds and the table. Young Tom climbed on top of the table to keep it from floating away, and held on for dear life to the ridgepole. I held the little ones on one bed and Artemus stood like a rock in the current, fending off debris that would have wrecked everything. Now we are all safe and dry. It was hard work shoveling out all the mud.

July 3, 1892

Today I received word that my dearest sister, India, has died back in Virginia. She had been sick for so long that her death is a blessing. Now she is in the Arms of the Lord and in no more pain. I will miss her more now, though, because I will have no more letters from her. They were getting less frequent as she weakened, and her penmanship was always poor. Artemus says we will never go back East, even though he is worn down with the mining. His efforts don't give us much gold to speak of. He loves the mountains, and so do I.

My List of Good Things

September 20, 1892

It has been a long time since I've kept up my list of blessings. I have had the mountain fever for the last six weeks. Young Tom has had to do for the younger ones and his father, and has turned into a good cook. In fact, Young Tom thinks he might become a cook for some mining camp. He doesn't cotton to the idea of being a miner down in a tunnel, or working in the placers where you always get wet. Sometimes the placer hoses get away from the men, and then the spray is like frozen hell, Artemus says. Men even get killed by the high-pressured hoses. So I'm pleased my boy has a direction to go in, even if it took me being so sick. And I had the most fascinating dreams in my fever! If only I could remember them I'm sure I would never lack for entertainment.

October 1, 1892

Effie Mondon, my best friend, has died. Her heart gave out, and her death was sudden, Mick said. I am thankful she didn't suffer but a minute. It was a blessing, I think. She hated it here, so now she can visit her folks Back East in spirit.

December 7, 1892

We finally have a house instead of a tent! Praise God. When the weather got too cold to work and the water froze so they couldn't use the placer hoses, the men got together and chopped some trees and built several small cabins. Those of us with young children had first pick. We are much warmer now. We even had a real glass window for awhile. Unfortunately, those poor motherless O'Shay children ran amuck and broke everyone's windows with stones. I covered the window with oiled paper and that keeps out most of the drafts. Those children even went into our cabin while I was away helping the Mondon young ones, and they broke my best blue willow dishes, all of them. I can't blame them because they have no one to teach them better. Their mother died on the trip West. I invited them and their overworked father for supper so they would see there were no hard feelings. We used tin plates. I wish I had more to give them, but I can't even have them over for supper again. We don't have nearly enough for our own brood.

February 5, 1893

Things have come full circle. Our new log cabin burned down, and we are back in our tent. The fire started when Young Tom was trying to cook up a mess of venison and bacon, and spilled the fat. The fire just got away from him. He feels so bad, but I tell him not to worry. We are all together and alive. We don't have a wooden floor for the rest of the winter, as the house burned to the dirt. It is hard to keep a dirt floor from turning to mud when it rains or snows, and it isn't as warm, but we manage. I am thankful that we saved our bedding. Artemus made us nice new rope beds with cedar posts pounded into the ground. We will build another house when the men can spare the time again next fall.

June 1, 1893

I greet the spring with joy. My list of blessings has grown long: The flowers are blooming and the breeze is warm. The raw skin on my hands (from doing laundry in cold water all winter) is nearly healed. And wonder of wonders! I am to have another baby sometime in the early fall. Life is hard, but it is a good life here in these beautiful mountains. My children are my dearest joy. Artemus is happy too, and he says that surely the men will hit a good vein of gold any day now.

Just This Once

Sherie Fox Schmauder

TWENTY-TWO
Just This Once

*A*nne Galen leaned out of the window of the stopped stagecoach and watched as the horse fought the reins, turning and backing and getting more tangled in the downed barbed wire of the open gate. The stagecoach driver and two men passengers ran to help the frantic rider. Blood was pumping from one of the horse's legs.

Looked like an artery was cut. Sighing, Anne reached for her medical bag, which she'd brought all the way from the East by force of habit, not that she'd planned on using it out West. She'd decided she would not be a doctor any more.

But this was a suffering animal. Just this once.

The gray gelding's coat had many gashes from the cruel wire. The men were able to free him, but he was still nearly uncontrollable from the pain.

"Hold him still," Anne called from a distance. "I'll stitch him up."

The men looked at her with astonishment. Her face beneath her piled dark brown hair was determined. She had removed her hat before she left the carriage, and she thought briefly of the blood that was going to stain her black traveling suit. Regrettable. In one hand she held the small kit containing her surgical equipment: silk thread, curved needles, forceps, lancets, scissors, alcohol.

"Stay back, Miss," the coach driver said. "He'll either stomp on you or get you all bloody, or both."

"I've had a horse since I was a child. I know animals," Anne answered absent-mindedly, fixing the horse with her ice-blue eyes.

Under her gaze, he began to calm down. She walked up to his head, breathed into his nostrils, and told him he was a good horse. She whispered she would help him, but he must be still. She gave him her hand to smell, and then ran it over his head and back along his sweaty mane. Bending down to the arterial flow on his right foreleg, she murmured gently as she tied a ligature above it. Then she swabbed the bloody area. Soon she could see where to stitch, and cleansed the area with alcohol. That hurt, and the horse danced a bit, but soon calmed.

The men were silent, the rider at the horse's head, the other men surrounding the animal. As Anne took the first stitch, the horse shuddered, but stood stock still.

"What is this beautiful animal's name?" she asked the rider.

"Smoky," the man said, still panting from his efforts to calm the horse.

Anne stitched rapidly, talking all the while to Smoky. When she was finished, she washed her hands in water from the driver's canteen, sponged off the worst of the bloodstains on her suit, replaced her hat, and suggested they get on with their trip to Fairplay.

"You a vet?" Smoky's rider asked. "I got no money, but if you'll tell me where I can find you, my boss will pay you."

"I'm not a vet. I'm good at stitching, that's all. This bag was my father's. You owe me nothing. Just promise to keep those wounds clean and don't ride him for several days. Lead him to where you're going."

♔

Thus began Anne Galen's life in Fairplay. Rumors abounded that she had a magic touch with animals, even if she said she wasn't a vet. People began appearing at the door of the small house she'd rented leading animals in various stages of distress, or with urgent calls to come attend a wayward cow birthing, or to treat an injured animal that couldn't be brought to her. Donkeys used by the mines were normally tended by the stock tenders, but they brought her their more serious cases. She always ended up saying, "Just this once."

Anne Galen knew it would be only a matter of time before she was called to treat humans. Some places had only vets to treat people. Yet she had sworn after that botched operation on her father that she would never again practice medicine.

The town's only physician, Dr. Weimar, had recently died of a destroyed liver due to alcoholism. Why couldn't doctors stop alcoholics from killing themselves? Why? . . . the list of things a doctor couldn't cure was endless.

And her father dead, of her own hand.

It was no surprise when she dreamed of him one cold winter night. She must go on, he said. It had been his time. Not her fault, only his for not knowing enough to teach her more. She would learn by doing.

Anne had sat bolt upright as the dream faded, and as she did, she was startled by a frenzied knocking on her door. It was a slim girl with a red shawl clutched tightly around her. Tears had streaked her eye makeup into black trails across her rouged cheeks.

"Please, Miss Galen, come quick, Charity's awful hurt. Evan Hunter beat her up. Madam says she'll die if you don't come."

"Just this once," Anne said. She struggled into a wool dress, threw on a coat, grabbed her bag and went out into the cold wind with the girl.

Charity would live. She wouldn't be pretty again, because of the broken facial bones and missing teeth. By the time Anne finished binding the girl's jaw, taping her broken nose straight and splinting her arm, it was daylight. A crowd of curious men watched her descend from the room above the bar. They all doffed their hats as she passed them. Some even said, "Thank you."

After that, Anne Galen accepted reluctantly the roll of doctor once again. She didn't tell anyone she had killed her father. They would find out her incompetence soon enough when she lost a few patients.

But the people of Fairplay didn't seem to blame her when every now and then one of her patients slipped away. Men wept when their wives died, but people didn't die often. Anne was fanatical about cleanliness, evidently in contrast to old Doc Weimar. He had been a crusty German, sloppy, using the alcohol to dull his senses instead of on his patients' wounds.

Anne began to think there was something about the clean air of the mountains — when the wind blew away the miasma and dust of the mines, that is — that helped her patients survive. She fought each illness, each injury, passionately. People learned to have boiling water ready, clean cloths available, a scrubbed table for her to operate on.

She set up a surgery in her front room, and hired Charity to be her helper. The girl thrived in this atmosphere, and said she was glad to be out of the saloon. Charity read the medical literature Anne sent away for, and soon became a good nurse. She wasn't squeamish at the operating table, even though grown men fainted dead away when watching operations.

Though she had told no one of the dream of her dead father, Anne began hearing tales of ghosts that frequented the mines and the mountains. People believed the stories so thoroughly that Anne decided she had better pay attention to them. Spirits were most active when deaths had been violent. Anne was called to advise the parents of a child who seemed to see apparitions and talk to them regularly, refusing to have anything to do with the living. She sent away for information on diseases of the mind.

Some women went mad after losing children or husbands. She heard tales of miners who came back to lead innocents out of storms and high mountains. Others told of Indian ghosts who bedeviled whites that had massacred their people.

Anne Galen came to believe that hiding crimes — and committing them in the first place — led to mental problems in some people. Perhaps she should tell everyone that she'd killed her own father. Yet she hadn't willfully killed him. She had been merely incompetent. She sent for books and articles on medicine; she learned new techniques.

No other doctors came to Fairplay, and she was busy from morning to night. Every time someone came to her door she thought, "Just this once." But that was an automatic response now, and she didn't even believe herself any more.

How could she leave the people of her town without anyone to help at all?

Her town. A wave of contentment swept over her. She straightened her shoulders, and leaned over to put another chunk of coal on the dying fire. The evening was turning dark this midsummer evening, and she must go to bed, hoping to sleep the night through without another call.

But instead of sleep, someone banged on her door.

The sheriff's deputy said, "Need you at the jail, Dr. Galen," he said. "Chinese woman injured a miner pretty bad. Their stories don't agree, but he probably had it coming. Don't see how she could have hurt him so bad. She's a tiny little thing. Arrested them both for assault."

Anne raised her eyebrows at that, but followed the man to the jail. The miner had several broken ribs and a broken leg. Bruises on his torso. Anne taped up the ribs, rubbed a good horse liniment on his bruises, and set the leg with splints. The morphine she gave him left him snoring.

In the next cell was a small Chinese woman sitting motionless on the cot. She had remained silent as the miner, yelping and crying out, had his injuries tended.

"Open the door, Sheriff," Anne demanded. "She must be injured too." She shooed the men out of the cellblock.

The woman gravely presented her body to Anne for examination. She was not injured at all. Her name was Ah Song, and her story was what Anne expected: the drunken man had set upon her as she walked down the street looking for a place to stay for the night.

"How did you injure this man so severely, and not be hurt yourself?"

"*Tai chi*," Ah Song said. "It is a practice that gives peace and strength to the body, and it is also a martial art, when needed. I killed with it once, and I did not want to kill this man. I have come back to the mountains to make my peace with the spirit of the one I did kill."

Anne Galen was astounded. This small woman had the strength to kill a grown man? "Can you show me how you do that?"

"You are not afraid to stand up to me? I will not hurt you, but you might be frightened."

Anne's smile showed her disbelief. "I'm not afraid." She looked around to be sure no one was listening at the door. Snores still came from the next cell. "I too killed a man, but from my own incompetence, not from my expertise. My father. You must tell no one."

"Your demons are your own, Doctor. My husband was killed by a man who then sought my body. I killed him to save myself, although I could no longer save my husband."

She stood up, and she barely came to Anne Galen's shoulder. Anne wondered if she should brace herself. But Ah Song said she would not hurt her.

"Try to knock me down," the small woman commanded. Anne was embarrassed, but she struck out suddenly to push the woman down on the bed.

Instead, she found herself flung down, but softly, as Ah Song cushioned her fall.

"There, you see, you did not expect that motion, and yet I could have killed you at any time." The woman wasn't even breathing heavily.

Anne sat up and smiled broadly. "I love it! If you were going to stay here I would ask you to teach me these things. All women should know this art. And I will speak to the judge for you, since you have been arrested for assault. It was in self-defense, obviously. You are a formidable woman, Ah Song."

Anne Galen took Ah Song to stay with her after the judge dismissed her charge. She heard the story of Ah Song's trek from China with her husband, her work on the railroad disguised as a boy, and her flight to a mining camp deep in the mountains after she had killed the man who murdered her husband. There in a laundry she had discovered how to glean gold from miners' dirty pants pockets. Now she had a successful import business in San Francisco.

The two women talked long into the nights about the medicine and philosophy of China. Telling Ah Song of how

Anne's father had died at her clumsy hands helped lay that painful memory to rest.

Ah Song began to teach Anne Galen and Charity *tai chi*. Listening to the young woman's story of her life in the brothel and her attack, Ah Song became obsessed with teaching Charity to defend herself. Her scars had given her a menacing look, but her former beauty still shone through. Men still looked at her on the street, but Ah Song's teaching diminished the shrinking, fearful way Charity had developed. Anne practiced with the two women when she had time.

Ah Song's trips into the mountains around Fairplay gave her peace. She took the mountains' solid presence into herself, just as Anne had accepted their strengthening influence. It was soon time for Ah Song to go back to her business in San Francisco.

Just this once, Anne thought after the Chinese woman had gone, just this once I wish I had someone like her for a friend. Then she realized she did have a friend here in Fairplay — Charity. They had medicine in common, and they both had needed healing from terrible experiences.

A vision of Ah Song practicing the graceful moves of her art came into Anne's mind, and she knew that Ah Song would always be her friend too.

And Anne Galen would always be a doctor. She had learned the science and the art of her craft. She had found a place where she cared for the people and they cared about her.

Everything was connected in this world. Ah Song had taught her that.